UNBRIDLED ANGER

Usually Melissa loved to linger over the clutter, the happy accumulation of a life lived with horses, but right now, all she could see as she barreled into Rose's office was the horrifying image of Angie, whipping AB while he cringed in fear.

"Melissa!" Rose exclaimed. "You're still here, kiddo? You should be on your way to school by now." She glanced at the horse clock on her wall, the one with the wooden tail that swished back and forth like a pendulum. "Correction. You should be *at* school. You haven't been alphabetizing the tack room, have you?"

Melissa closed her eyes and gritted her teeth, waiting for the anger to pass. It didn't.

"Melissa, dear, what on earth has got you so riled?"

"Angie." She nearly spat out the name.

"Ah. Well, she's not particularly my favorite person, either."

"Rose, she just beat AB." Melissa fought back tears, remembering the horse's look of terror. "You've got to do something!"

Titles in the Silver Creek Riders *series*

SILVER CREEK RIDERS

Winning

Beth Kincaid

JOVE BOOKS, NEW YORK

SILVER CREEK RIDERS: WINNING

A Jove Book / published by arrangement with
the author

PRINTING HISTORY
Jove edition / February 1995

All rights reserved.
Copyright © 1995 by Jove Publications, Inc.
Cover illustration by Patty Cosgrove.
This book may not be reproduced in whole
or in part, by mimeograph or any other means,
without permission. For information address:
The Berkley Publishing Group, 200 Madison Avenue,
New York, New York 10016.

ISBN: 0-515-11499-5

A JOVE BOOK®
Jove Books are published by The Berkley Publishing Group,
200 Madison Avenue, New York, New York 10016.
JOVE and the "J" design are trademarks belonging
to Jove Publications, Inc.

PRINTED IN THE UNITED STATES OF AMERICA

10 9 8 7 6 5 4 3 2

1

The sign over the new shop was calling out to her.

MANE STREET EMPORIUM
For the well-dressed equestrian
and the well-dressed horse

Melissa! Melissa Hall! it beckoned. *Spend that allowance money here! Indulge! Who needs school supplies, anyway?*

Melissa grabbed her friend's arm. "Jenna. I'm begging you. Stop me before I spend again."

Jenna McCloud pressed her nose against the window. "They've got a new shipment of breeches on sale, Melissa. White, buff, brown, gray, rust—and yes, even canary."

"Stop tempting her," Katie Anderson scolded. She joined Jenna at the window. "Hey, and hunt coats," she added. "Perfect for the Autumn Horse Show."

"Can it, you two," Melissa said firmly. She unfolded the list she'd typed up that morning. "Number two pencils," she recited. "Recycled paper, preferably college ruled. You can get more on the page that way.

1

Locker shelf organizer. Calculator, solar powered. Pen. Erasable, if possible. And supplies for my photography class." Melissa jerked her thumb toward the store across the street. "I'm going to Daley's Office Supply. They'll have most of this stuff."

"Yeah," Jenna said, "but does Daley's have leather riding gloves at twenty percent off?"

"You are evil. Quite possibly satanic." Melissa shoved the list in her jeans pocket. She gazed into the window. "Are they thermal lined?"

"There's only one way to find out." Jenna pushed open the glass door and a bell tinkled. The smell of new leather was tantalizing. Melissa pursed her lips.

"I've got you now, my pretty!" Jenna said, holding the door wide.

Seconds later, Melissa was browsing through a selection of wool riding coats. Jenna made a beeline for the velvet hunt caps, while Katie browsed through a display of white ratcatcher blouses.

"Can I help you with anything?" asked a young girl with a large wad of gum in her freckled cheek.

"Nope," Melissa said. "Just browsing."

"We've got a whole other room with tack."

"We don't own horses . . . yet," Jenna said. She popped a too-large hard hat on her head. Her short brown hair disappeared from view. "But we all take lessons at Silver Creek Stable together. Does this come in petite?"

"Maybe your brain will grow," Katie said. "There's hope through research."

"Hey, don't take it out on me just because you have to special-order your hard hats from the mega-head catalog," Jenna sniffed.

Melissa laughed. A typical Jenna-Katie exchange. Despite their differences, the two of them had been best friends since they were little kids. Jenna was a pint-sized force of nature who talked at the speed of light and got into trouble even faster. Katie was tall and lanky (too tall and lanky, she complained), with long curly black hair that she wore in a ponytail all the time. She was shy and sensitive, a quiet balance to Jenna's occasional outrageousness.

"I don't know much about those hat thingies," the clerk admitted. "We just opened a little while ago and I'm not exactly . . . you know. Horsey. My last job I worked at Taco Bell. Filling burritos, mostly." She reached into her pocket for a fresh piece of gum. "So where is this Silver Creek, anyway?"

"It's the stable over by the state park," Melissa said. "Near the middle school, right off Twin Oaks Road."

"Listen to Melissa," Jenna said. "She's a certified local already."

Melissa grinned. Truth was, she was starting to *feel* like a local, although she'd only moved to this tranquil area in upstate New York a few months ago.

"Isn't there a horse camp over at Silver Creek?" the clerk asked.

"In the summer," Melissa said. She pulled out a riding coat and slipped it on. "That's where we all met, actually."

What a surprise that had turned out-to be. As one of the few African-Americans at the camp, Melissa had expected to feel like an outsider all summer. Instead she'd ended up having the best riding camp experience of her life—and making some wonderful new friends.

"Horse camp, huh?" the salesgirl mused. "I spent the summer watching *All My Children* and eating Cheetos."

"We spent the whole summer together in a big, old tent that smelled like a goat," Katie added.

"And mucked out stalls," Jenna said, sighing.

"And picked hoofs," Melissa added.

The salesgirl curled her lip. "This is your idea of a summer vacation?"

"It was amazing," Jenna said. "Riding, every single day."

Melissa nodded. "I'm already going through withdrawal."

The salesgirl rolled her eyes. "I just don't get horse people," she said, sauntering off.

"Maybe she should reconsider a career in burritos," Jenna whispered.

Katie fingered through a rack of down-filled nylon trail vests. "You can't understand how great riding camp is unless you've done it," she said wistfully.

"I miss it, don't you?" Melissa said. "It's not going to be the same, just going for lessons once a week."

"I miss Sharon, too," Katie said.

Sharon Finnerty had been the fourth member of their tent. A fourteen-year-old former riding champion, her legs had been badly injured in an accident that had claimed the life of her horse. "I know she just lives a few miles from us, but with her going to a private school, she might as well be in a foreign country. Who knows what the Breton Academy's like? They might have different customs."

"Maybe we could hire a translator, in case there's a language barrier," Jenna suggested.

"As long as Sharon speaks horse, nothing will change," Melissa said. "We'll see her at Silver Creek all the time. That's what really counts." She examined her reflection in a full-length mirror. "You know, it's funny. Normally I'd be a nervous wreck about starting a new school, but having you guys and Silver Creek to count on, I'm not even worried. Well, I'm not losing sleep nights, at least. Having riding to count on makes me feel secure, you know?" She spun around. "So what do you think?"

Katie nodded approval. "You look like you're ready to accept the championship ribbon at the Autumn Horse Show."

The clerk wandered back in and blew a larger-than-life bubble. Jenna moved to pop it but Katie held her back. "Looks nice," the clerk said to Melissa. "Fifteen percent off, too."

"I can't," Melissa said, shucking off the coat. "It would wipe out my savings." She hesitated. "Still, it *is* a big show . . ."

"A big horse show?" the salesgirl asked.

"At the end of the month at Willow Brook Riding

Center," Katie explained. "It's our first accredited show. Well, mine and Jenna's. Melissa's a more experienced rider."

"So that's, like, a big deal?"

"Major big deal," Jenna confirmed.

Jenna held up a baseball cap. *I'd Rather Be Riding* was embroidered on the brim. "Does this come in petite?"

"Search me," said the clerk.

Melissa slipped the coat onto the rack. A moment later, she snatched it back. "You know, I could always put it on hold and then discuss it with my mom. Maybe we could go halfsies."

She knew that money had been a little tight since her parents' recent divorce. Still, the coat was on sale, and she'd definitely outgrown her old one. It was uncomfortable in the shoulders, and her mom wouldn't want her trying to jump all cramped up, would she?

Besides, she did look good in it. Very, blue ribbon, good.

"I think you've got a live one over there," Jenna said to the clerk.

"A what?"

"A live one. You know. A sale."

"Not a sale," Melissa said firmly. "A pre-sale." She handed the coat to the clerk. "Could you hold this for me for a day or two? I need to have my mom come in and take a look at it."

"But first she needs to butter her up," Katie added.

"That's not how my mom and I operate," Melissa said. "We have a very egalitarian relationship. We respect each other. I will just calmly explain the facts in a logical, reasonable, unemotional manner. I'll say, 'Mom, my old coat is too small, and I have an important show coming up.' "

Jenna crossed her arms. "And how about when that doesn't work?"

"Then I'll get down on my knees and beg like a dog."

"Very egalitarian," Katie said.

They followed the clerk to the counter. She frowned at the coat, considering.

"What's wrong?" Melissa asked.

"That whole mucking out thing," she said. "I just don't get it. I mean, this is such a nice coat. Why do you guys, like, wear formalwear while you pick up the horse poop?"

As always, Melissa's mom had left a note for her on the kitchen table.

Quote for the day:
One morning I shot an elephant in my pajamas.
How he got into my pajamas I don't know.
      —Groucho Marx in Animal Crackers
(Funny movie, even if it is prehistoric. Remind me to rent it for us sometime.)
      —M.

Melissa laughed. For as long as she could remember, her mom had been leaving notes like this for Melissa and her brother Thomas to read when they got home from school.

The answering machine showed one call. Melissa pushed the play button as she began loading dishes in the dishwasher.

"Melissa? Hi, it's me, Sharon. How was the shopping expedition? Sorry I missed it. Nothing new at my doc. She just wanted to check out my braces and hassle me about overdoing it, the usual. I can't believe school starts tomorrow, can you? Hey, is this one of those machines that cuts you off or is that Katie's? I can never remember. . . . I'm so low-tech. Well, anyway. Guess that's it. Talk to you later."

When Melissa was done with the dishes, she cleared the kitchen table of its pile of thick, attic-smelling books. Her mother worked as a reporter for the local paper, but in her spare time she was doing research for a book on the lives of important twentieth-century black women in the U.S. No matter how hard she worked all day, at night she came home and poured her soul into the project she called "her baby." Sometimes at night she would get so excited about some obscure fact she'd resurrected that she'd rouse Melissa from her sleep to say, "Melissa, listen to what I just discovered!" And Melissa would listen and nod and think what a really cool mom she had and then fall instantly back to sleep.

Melissa wrapped a rubber band around a handful

of her mother's index cards. Her mom was the slob to end all slobs, which was probably why Melissa was so obsessively neat. It was self-defense. She wouldn't let her mother near her territory, near her color-coded sock drawer and her alphabetized bathroom cabinet. It wasn't that, like lots of other girls, she had some secret diary to hide. Melissa didn't have any secrets from her mom, not really. It was just that she didn't want her mother creating a natural disaster in her pristine room.

She moved a pile of the steno notebooks her mother used for reporting at the city desk. She'd worked at a much bigger paper in Maryland, but after the divorce, Ms. Hall had wanted to move back to the area she'd grown up in, and she'd settled for work at the local paper, the *Silver Creek Gazette*.

As she piled and arranged, Melissa was formulating a plan. She would make her mom's favorite dinner, vegie lasagna. Not as a bribe, which is what Jenna and Katie would undoubtedly say it was. But if, as her mother was eating, she just happened to remark on what a fine and responsible daughter Melissa was, well, that would make an opportune moment to mention that new tack shop and that very reasonably priced riding coat . . . And in any case, her mom had seemed a little tired lately. Making dinner was the least Melissa could do.

As Melissa stuffed a pile of newspapers into the wastebasket, she hesitated. There were yellow highlighter marks on a bunch of want ads. Cars?

Could it be her mom was actually going to dump Freddie K, the rusty heap that, like the hero of all those horror movies, never quite seemed to die?

She scanned the ads. These were employment ads. Why would her mom be looking at ads for jobs? She loved her work at the *Gazette*, even if she did like to complain about covering local events like the Little Miss Walleye Pike pageant.

A job for a part-time restaurant hostess was highlighted. Sales clerk, temporary part-time. The Burger Barn was looking for line cooks.

Line cooks? Her mother thought microwaving fish sticks was a culinary challenge. What was going on?

Melissa stared at the clock on the stove. Her mother would get off work at five, then pick up eight-year-old Thomas at his karate lesson. She'd could make the lasagna, call Sharon, and still have plenty of time left over to worry.

Melissa had to wait until dinner was over and Thomas was safely ensconced in front of the computer. She followed her mother into her bedroom and cleared a spot out of the jumble of dirty clothes and magazines on her mother's bed.

"We need to talk," Melissa said.

"Oh?" Her mother was sorting through a pile of earrings on her dresser, searching for a matching hoop. "About school? You worried, honey?"

"No, Mom. I mean, yes, I am worried, a little, but

that's not what we need to talk about."

"Why is it you're starting to sound way too much like my mother?" Ms. Hall asked. "Or—uh-oh—is it *me* you're starting to sound like?"

"I found the want ads."

"The—oh. I wondered where those went." Her mother's shoulders sagged.

"You can imagine my surprise," Melissa said sternly, "when I saw that you'd circled the job as graveyard shift donut maker. I mean, come on, Mom. You can't even make toast without a cookbook and a fire extinguisher. And then there's that other little matter."

"You mean I'd eat all the donuts," her mother said nonchalantly.

"I *mean* the last I heard, you had a job." Melissa clutched her mother's pillow to her chest, waiting.

Ms. Hall sank down onto the bed. It was like looking into a mirror, a few more lines, a few gray hairs, but they shared the same almond eyes and smile that turned down a bit at the corners. Her mother was so pretty that, even on her worst zit and grungy hair days, Melissa always reminded herself she couldn't grow up to look too bad, not with her mom's genes.

But there was something in her mother's face now that scared Melissa. Not fear—her mom never seemed afraid of anything, with the possible exception of large spiders.

It was something else. She looked tired. She looked resigned.

"You lost your job, didn't you, Mom?"

"Not lost, exactly. More like misplaced temporarily. Something about belt-tightening."

"But you just started at the paper," Melissa said reasonably. Her mother was a good reporter. It didn't make sense, and she hated it when things didn't make sense.

"Last hired, first fired. But they promised I'll be the first rehired. It may only be a few months. And the good news is, I get to work for another week. And my supervisor promised to give me a swell you're-fired-get-lost party."

She flopped back on the bed and reached out for Melissa's hand. Melissa took it and squeezed.

"You're squeezing awfully hard," her mother said after a while. "Is that a gesture of solidarity, or are you PO'ed at me?"

Melissa withdrew her hand. "How long have you known?"

"Just this past week." She rolled onto her side. "Oh, so that's it. I know, Lissa, I should have told you right away. But this last year it seems like all I've been is the bearer of bad tidings. First, the divorce, then the move. I just didn't want to have to tell you this, too. A triple whammy. I don't know, maybe I just didn't want to have to say it out loud myself."

"You should have told me. You always say we're a team. We're in this together. All for one and one for all." Melissa found a matching pair of clean socks and rolled them into a tight ball. "I'm really disappointed in you, Mom."

"You *do* sound like Grandma Tyler. It's uncanny. Although you scare me more."

Melissa started on another pair.

"Come on, not even a little smile?"

"I'm serious, Mom."

"Lissa, listen to me." Her mother's voice had that ice-cream smooth tone she got when she was deadly serious. "You've been through a lot this year. You've lost your old friends and you've had to make new ones. You had to break up with Marcus. You had to change stables. You had to move from the house you grew up in to this postage stamp they pretend is an apartment. And," she sighed, staring up at the ceiling, "well, I know how much you miss your dad. I just didn't want to lay any more crap on you right now. Being an eighth-grader is a full-time job. When I was in eighth grade, it felt like a job and a half. Of course, I wasn't as together as you are. Actually, I was pretty much a complete geek."

"I'm not so together." Melissa said it quietly.

"You seem that way. Sometimes you seem so together it worries me. I mean, I'm supposed to be the mom in this relationship."

Melissa gazed at her reproachfully.

"So what is it you want?" her mother cried in exasperation. "You want me to lay the whole grim picture on you? You want me to drag you down into the depths with me? You want me to turn you into a dispirited adult before your time? You want . . ." She grinned. "You wanna go make some popcorn?"

"Yes!" Melissa cried. "And while we do, you'll tell me all the horrible details?"

"Everything," her mother vowed, sounding vaguely mystified. "And maybe later, for an extra good time, you can help me work out a new austerity budget."

"Wonderful," Melissa said, at last feeling useful. "I'm much better at numbers than you. Maybe we should computerize it. I could make some graphs—"

"Melissa, sometimes you amaze me. What did I do to deserve such a cool kid?"

"Well, you're a pretty cool mom. For a former geek."

Her mother stood and held out her arms. "For starters, you can help by giving me a hug."

Melissa climbed off the bed and wrapped her arms around her mom.

"You sure you're okay?" her mother whispered.

"I am now. No more secrets, okay?"

"Promise." Her mother kissed the top of her head. "Maybe I should reread that parenting book. *Amazing, Agonizing Adolescence*, wasn't that what it was called? I feel like I'm failing you somehow."

"You're not. You're my best friend."

"Mine too."

"We'll be okay, Mom."

Her mother didn't speak. Melissa could hear her heart surging gently, reassuringly, a soothing counterpoint to the blood racing through her own temples.

"Lissa?" her mother said. For the first time, there were tears in her voice. "You know what this means about lessons, don't you, hon?"

"I know, Mom. It's okay." Melissa broke free of her mother's arms. "I'd better do the popcorn," she said lightly. "You always burn it."

2

It was a first-rate dream. Soundtrack courtesy of MTV, colors by Disney. Sharon was riding a beautiful Thoroughbred the color of midnight along an immaculate beach. A guy was galloping alongside her on an equally magnificent bay. The guy was nameless and faceless, but had very white teeth. And he was just about to declare his undying devotion.

Unfortunately, every time he opened his mouth, the phone rang.

Resentfully, Sharon flailed out her arm. On the third try, she found the receiver.

"Make it good," she muttered.

"This is your morning wake-up call!" The disturbingly chirpy voice could only belong to Katie.

Sharon closed her eyes. If she tried, she could still resurrect a fleeting glimpse of the guy with the teeth . . .

"Sharon?" Katie half-covered the receiver. "She just lapsed back into her coma."

The phone changed hands. "Wake up, Finnerty!"

"Beat it, Jenna," Sharon moaned, burrowing into her pillow. "I'm in the middle of an oceanfront gallop with a miraculously cute guy."

"I think she forgot her medication again," Jenna whispered to Katie.

"He's deeply devoted to me. Even if I don't know his name. And he flosses regularly."

"This is it, Sharon! Day one of school. And more importantly, our first riding lesson since camp ended. Aren't you excited?"

"School, no. Lesson, yes." Sharon yawned. "Wait a minute. How come you're so perky, anyway? Do you have any idea what time it is?"

"I spent the night at Katie's. She woke me up an hour ago so I could help her decide which pair of jeans to wear to school. The Levi's with the knee-hole won."

"Well, thanks for the fashion bulletin." Sharon moved to drop the receiver, but Jenna, as usual, was still talking.

"We already called Melissa," she said. "She was in a bad mood, though."

"I can relate."

"Worse than you, I mean."

"May I be excused now?"

"Just a minute. Katie wants to talk to you." A moment's fumbling, then, "Sharon? See you at Silver Creek after school, okay?"

"Katie?"

"Yeah?"

"You're not going to pull this stunt every morning, are you?"

Sharon dropped the receiver and snuggled down

under her comforter. It was cold for early September. Not see-your-breath cold, like it would have been back in Vermont, where she'd lived before moving here. But cold enough to make showering an intimidating prospect.

She closed her eyes and tried to conjure up white-teeth. He was just galloping up to rejoin her when the phone rudely interrupted.

Jenna and Katie again. Sharon grabbed it on ring two. "Why is it you keep bugging me just when things start getting interesting?" she demanded.

"Oh . . . oh, I'm really sorry." The girl on the other end sounded genuinely embarrassed. "I didn't mean to . . . This *is* the Finnerty residence, isn't it?"

"Yep. But I have the strange feeling you aren't Jenna and Katie, are you?"

"Neither one." The girl laughed. "My name is Marta Aritas. I'm trying to reach Sharon Finnerty."

"You've reached her, all right. And she's slightly embarrassed. Actually, she'd be more embarrassed, but she's half-asleep."

"Listen, I'm sorry to call so early. I was so excited about this assignment, and I've got an early class at the community college . . . I figured this would be a good time to catch up with you."

Sharon rubbed her eyes and sat up. "Assignment, did you say?"

"Sorry. I guess I should start at the beginning. I'm a journalism major and I intern part-time at the *Silver Creek Gazette*. Anyway, they're giving me my first assignment—it's for the youth page, actually. You know, where they run stories about kids in the community?"

"Are you sure you've got the right number?"

"Absolutely," Marta said. "Ms. Hall told me about you—"

"Melissa's mom?"

"That's right. She said you and her daughter were friends. And anyway, she told me about your—you know"—Marta lowered her voice—"your unfortunate accident and all, and how you're riding again and about to compete in your first accredited show since—you know—and I thought what a great human interest story it would make."

"I'm sorry, Marta," Sharon replied. "I guess I don't exactly see why anybody in his right mind would want to read about my . . . you know."

"But it's perfect, don't you see?" Marta said enthusiastically. "Triumph over adversity. Tragedy and pain, fighting the odds. People eat that up."

"I don't think so."

"But you'd be an inspiration to others, Sharon."

"I'm really not inspiration material. Trust me."

Marta fell quiet. Sharon could hear the nervous tap-tap-tap of a pencil eraser.

"So, anyway," Sharon said. "Thanks for asking. I'll look forward to seeing your byline—"

"See, there's something else," Marta said meekly. "I sort of already sort of promised my editor I was doing this story. They sort of already have a photographer assigned and everything. I guess I screwed up. Sort of."

It was Sharon's turn to be quiet.

She had no desire whatsoever to dredge up the past.

Besides, how many readers of the *Gazette* could actually relate to her story? How many had suffered through a tragic car accident where their legs had been severely damaged and their horse killed?

On the other hand, this Marta girl sounded awfully desperate.

And it was remotely possible—just remotely—that if Sharon shared her story, it might actually end up doing some good.

Sharon exhaled slowly. "Will this take long?" she finally asked.

"No!" Marta said hopefully. "I promise."

"And I don't have to tell you my innermost secrets or anything, do I?"

"Of course not."

"Not that I have any innermost secrets," Sharon said. "I don't even have any outermost secrets. But if I did, I wouldn't want to share them with the entire population of greater Miller Falls. Not to mention Pooleville."

"So you'll do it?"

"Yeah, I suppose."

"Great. Wonderful. This is so cool. Could we meet in town this afternoon?"

"I've got a lesson after school. How about tomorrow

at McCloud Nine?" Sharon suggested. The little restaurant Jenna's family owned seemed like safe, neutral territory. "Four-thirtyish?"

"Perfect," Marta said triumphantly, sounding like she'd just locked up an exclusive interview with the President. "I'm thinking we might even do a follow-up story after the Autumn Horse Show, too. You know, watch your triumphant return to the ring? Well, see you this afternoon."

"I don't think—" Sharon began, but Marta had already hung up, leaving an irritating dial tone in her wake.

Sharon stared at the receiver in disbelief. What had she just gotten herself into? She should never, ever answer the phone first thing in the morning. If she'd been more awake, she would never have caved so easily.

Truth was, she wouldn't even *have* the luxury of a phone in her bedroom, except that her bedroom had actually been the living room in a former life. After her accident, she'd had to move down here to avoid the unnecessary complication of the stairs. Her father had remodeled the downstairs bath to accommodate Sharon's wheelchair, back before she'd graduated to a walker, and then to braces. Even now, the bathtub was equipped with a special chair Sharon could sit in.

She stared at the wall facing her bed. The shrine, her thirteen-year-old brother Sean called it. Ribbons plastered every square inch like garish wallpaper. Her dresser and a table were weighted down with trophies glittering like fool's gold, which was what, in the end, it had turned out to be.

On her nightstand was the check her mom had written, the entry fee for the Autumn Horse Show at Willow Brook. Sharon was signing up for the walk/trot class. Sharon Finnerty, Champion at the New England Classic, on-her-way-to-the-Olympics Sharon Finnerty, reduced to a walk/trot class.

She would never be that Sharon again. Her friends at camp had helped her begin to accept that reality. But it was one thing to accept it privately, to ride among a few friends at camp or in her small class at Silver Creek. It was quite another to ride publicly in a big show, to let the whole world see how much she'd changed. And how much she'd lost.

Her triumphant return to the ring. Hardly. Old Marta, cub reporter, was in for a rude awakening.

That afternoon, Melissa took Big Red around the ring at a slow sitting trot. She'd tacked up in a furious rush, so fast she'd left Jenna and Katie behind in the stable. Three other girls were already moving around the ring. Melissa knew them all from camp—Louisa Tisch, Erin Casey, and Becca Wallace, but she'd barely done more than nod a quick hello. She had other things on her mind today.

Today she wanted to savor every possible minute of riding. This might be her last ride on a horse for a very long time, and Melissa was determined to make every moment count.

She began to post. She no longer gave any thought to finding her diagonal or maintaining her position. When Red's outside shoulder moved, she rose without thinking, legs still, hands steady, weight dropping into her heels. Everything on automatic, every move coming from some part of her that had nothing to do with the logical, orderly Melissa she was the rest of the time.

Not that riding didn't require intense concentration. It did. But when you were *on*, when you were having a good day and you and your horse were really communicating, riding was about more than rational thought. It wasn't brain-work, like taking a test at school. It was about something deeper, something almost mystical.

And now, at least for a while, she would have to learn to get by without it.

"Why isn't she talking to us?" Katie asked loudly as she entered the ring on Blooper, the world's gentlest bay gelding.

"Because Melissa is in eighth grade, whereas we are lowly seventh-graders and therefore less highly evolved," Jenna replied. "In the great Silver Creek Middle School hierarchy, we are worm slime. We are bathtub scum. We are tooth decay."

"She ate lunch with us today," Katie pointed out.

"She was just slumming. Taunting us with her superior status."

Melissa smiled but didn't answer. She was trying

to soak it all in, to take a mental photo with all five
senses. The rich, warm smell of the horses. The gentle
groan of the leather saddle as she moved. The play of
the sun on Red's coat, painting it with glints of gold.
The taste of the fall air, hinting of early shadows and
cider and pine. And most of all the feel, the heat,
the surge of muscle beneath her, the ballet at her
command.

"Turbo's sure feisty today," Jenna commented.

Melissa glanced over her shoulder. Jenna was
riding the magnificent chestnut gelding Silver Creek
had purchased that summer. Jenna had planned to
buy Turbo herself, but money problems at home had
intervened.

Melissa clenched her reins. Jenna hadn't hesitated
to tell anyone who would listen about the way her
parents had been strapped for cash. When they couldn't
buy Turbo, Jenna had been perfectly honest about her
disappointment.

So why was it that Melissa hadn't been able to
bring herself to tell her friends about her mother's
job loss?

Because, Melissa told herself, it would have meant
saying the words out loud—*I can't ride anymore.*

You might as well say I can't be me anymore, she
thought. *That I will, from now on, be an entirely
different person, a person who doesn't ride, who doesn't
have horses at the very center of her existence.*

Funny. Today had been Melissa's first day at a
brand-new school. A brand-new, not exactly ethnically

diverse school, to boot. But she had soared through it. Partly it was because she'd had Jenna and Katie there as anchors. They'd met before school, sat together at lunch, waved in the hall.

But surviving school had also been easier because Melissa had known at the end of the day she would have this moment to look forward to. That's how riding had always been for her—the one thing that she could always count on in a not always reliable world.

Sharon came walking up the long drive toward the ring. She was carrying a backpack and wearing a long colorful skirt that helped hide the slight lurch in her steps. Dangling turquoise and silver earrings hung from her ears, and her wild red hair had been tamed into submission with an antique silver barrette.

"One year, nine months, three days, four hours twenty seven minutes," Sharon muttered.

"What's going to happen in one year, etcetera, etcetera?" Jenna asked.

Sharon dropped her backpack. "That's how long till I get my learner's permit. Why is it none of us can drive yet? That bus, which, incidentally, smells remarkably like the boys' locker room, takes forever to get here."

"How do you know?" Kate asked.

"Because I just rode on it, obviously."

"No. How do you know what the boys' locker room smells like?"

Sharon gave a devious grin, but before she could answer, Margaret Stone, an instructor at Silver Creek who also doubled as the stable's bookkeeper, came dashing up. "Hey, gang!" she called. "We need to talk about the Autumn Horse Show at the Willow Brook. Moolah time." She opened a large blue notebook, brushing her short blond hair out of her eyes as she scanned a page crowded with names.

Melissa and the others slowed their horses and gathered by the fence. "Some of you have already paid your entrance fees and sent in your applications. I'm trying to organize the rest of the Silver Creek contingent. Let's see . . . Louisa, you're all set. Also Katie and Becca."

"I've got my check in here somewhere," Sharon said, digging through her backpack.

"Melissa, Jenna and Erin, the deadline's next Saturday, don't forget. You can send your application in directly, or I can take care of it."

"I—" Melissa began, but the words evaporated.

Margaret looked over at her. "Question, Melissa?"

"No," Melissa said quickly. "Nothing."

A regal palomino stepped out of the stable, his creamy gold coat catching the sunlight. On his back was a girl, maybe sixteen or so, with sleek blond chin-length hair and light blue, appraising eyes.

"Angie?" Margaret called. "I'm sending in show applications and checks. You want to add yours?"

"Thanks, Margaret, that'd be great."

"Have you all met Angie Marquette?" Margaret asked. "She's a new boarder."

"Actually, AB is the new boarder," Angie said with

a laugh as she rode over. "AB, for Arkansas Breeze."

"What a beauty," Sharon said, stroking the palomino's satiny white mane.

"I just got him a few months ago," Angie said. "He's a handful." She laughed again. "Lately, I've had an easier time learning to drive my mom's stick-shift."

"See?" Sharon said, throwing up her hands. "She has a car. Proof, as if you needed it, that life is not fair."

"She has a horse, too," Jenna added with grin. "That's really proof."

"You guys ever need a ride when I'm here, just give a yell," Angie said.

"Horse or car?" Sharon joked.

"Either one," Angie said. She legged AB into a brisk collected trot and headed off toward the main trail behind the stable buildings.

"She seemed nice," Jenna said.

"Nice *and* mobile, too," Sharon added.

Claire Donovan, an instructor whose mother owned the stable, came out of the office and waved. "Hey, Sharon!" she called. "Guess who I just talked to? Some girl named Marta."

"Oh, man." Sharon slumped against the fence.

"Who's Marta?" Jenna asked.

"An intern at the *Gazette*," Claire replied as she approached the group. She put her arm around Sharon, an act that required her to stand on tiptoes. "She wants the scoop on our little celebrity for an article about how Sharon's getting back into riding. And since I'm the head instructor here at Silver Creek, she thought I could provide the real dope."

"You are looking at the real dope," Sharon moaned. "I cannot believe I told that girl yes. She sounded so desperate, and I was half-asleep . . . I agreed to meet her tomorrow at McCloud Nine for an interview. Will you three come along for moral support?"

"Are you kidding?" Jenna said. "We wouldn't miss it for the world. Besides, I promised my mom I'd bus tables tomorrow."

"I think this is wonderful, Sharon," Katie said. "It'll be inspirational."

"Yeah, that's me. Inspiration central." Sharon cocked an eye at Claire. "What did you tell her, anyway?"

"Actually, I told her you were one of the strongest persons I'd ever met—in the ring, or outside of it."

Sharon blushed, an occurrence about as rare as a sighting of Halley's comet. "Claire's right, Sharon," Melissa said with feeling. "I mean, I've known you as a competitor and as a friend." Two years ago, Melissa had competed against Sharon at the New England Classic, a major show where she'd been the reserve champion to Sharon's champion.

"I just wish I'd said no," Sharon said regretfully. "But I guess it's too late now."

"Come on," Claire chided. "It might turn out to be fun. Remember how reluctant you were to help train Luna this summer? Look how great that turned out."

Luna was a skittish dapple gray filly Claire had

volunteered to lunge-train for a friend. She'd talked Sharon into helping out, and although it had taken a long time to gain the filly's trust, it had been a wonderful experience.

"I can deal with horses," Sharon said. "It's people who make me nervous."

"You know, I got a letter from Tony, my friend who owns Luna. He said he cannot believe how much she's transformed."

"I kind of miss her," Sharon admitted. "I knew when summer ended he was going to pick her up, but every time I go into the stable, I expect to see her silly little face peering over the door."

"Good thing. Tony's thinking of sending her back here for some more training down the road." Claire grinned. "Trust me, Sharon. If you can handle a filly that troublesome, you can handle some reporter. Besides, you're going to be a local celebrity. Can a shot on *Oprah* and *Sally Jesse* be far behind?"

"I gotta go tack up," Sharon said. "Suddenly I'm feeling nauseous." She turned to leave, then paused. "Oh. I almost forgot. My mom's going to be a few minutes late picking us up today, guys."

"Whose turn is it next lesson to pick up?" Katie asked. "Melissa's or mine?"

"Um, that reminds me," Melissa said, stroking Big Red's mane distractedly. "My mom can't do pick-up anymore. For a while, anyway. She's got to, uh, work late for a few weeks."

"No prob," Jenna said. "My mom loves to cart us

around. She says it's the only chance she ever gets to leave the restaurant."

Melissa smiled weakly.

"Okay, enough chat," Claire said firmly. "Don't forget, after today we're moving to lessons on Saturday at ten sharp, no excuses. Now, I want everybody tacked up and warmed up in ten minutes. We've got a lot of work to do before the big show. And I do mean a *lot* of work."

Melissa turned Red away, fighting back tears. There wasn't going to be a show for her, not this time.

She gazed wistfully at the wide rolling fields beyond the stable. Trails crisscrossed Silver Creek's land like ribbons on a package. Beyond a ridge of thick pines loomed Lookout Mountain, the highest point in Silver Creek State Park, its craggy outline blurred by the afternoon haze.

In the nearest field, Angie streaked past on AB. She was kicking him hard, thrusting her heels deep into the poor horse's ribs again and again. If she wanted more speed, why wasn't she relying more on her seat and her legs and less on the heels of her boots? Next time Melissa saw Angie, maybe she'd offer some pointers.

The realization fell over her like a shadow on the sun.

There wasn't going to be a next time.

3

"What is that goop? Snot stew?"

Melissa stared into the pot simmering on the front burner. "Would that be more evidence of that sparkling third-grade wit?"

Thomas sniffed at the pot, his skateboard under one arm. "Oh, man, it's macaroni and cheese again? We had that last night."

"And you'd better get used to it." Melissa turned the burner to low. She still had on her dusty breeches and muddy boots, but she wanted to get dinner started before her mom got home. Today was the day of her "you're fired" party at work, and Melissa knew she'd need some moral support. Unfortunately, leftover mac and cheese was hardly the ultimate pick-me-up.

Thomas scanned the note their mother had left on the table.

Quote for the day:
  The ultimate measure of a man is not where he
  stands in moments of comfort and convenience,
  but where he stands at times of challenge and
  controversy.
                                    —*Martin Luther King, Jr.*

"I don't get it," Thomas said.

"It means when the going gets tough, the tough get going," Melissa said, yanking off her boots.

"I still don't get it." With the palm of his hand, Thomas spun the wheels on his skateboard. He had that scrunched-up look he got when he was deep in thought. "Lissa," he said suddenly, "are we going to be poor?"

"Mom'll get another job eventually," Melissa assured him gently. "We'll be fine. We just have to tighten our belts for a while."

"Like no more allowance?"

"Yeah. And no more griping when you have to eat snot stew ten days running. And you can probably cross those new Nikes you've been drooling over off your list."

She thought of the riding coat at Mane Street Emporium. She could cross that off, too. Oh, well. She wasn't going to be riding in the big show. What did it matter?

The front door opened and they heard their mother's cheerful hello. "Melissa, you saint. You cooked."

"Close. I reheated."

Ms. Hall kicked off her shoes and sank into a chair. "Hey, guy," she said to Thomas. "How was the first day of school?"

"Okay. Mr. Chapple's pretty cool for an old guy, but he gave us a math test. Our first day, can you believe it?"

"How'd you do?"

"You know what?" Thomas said, eyes bright. "I've been meaning to take out that trash."

"Uh-huh," Ms. Hall said as he ran to grab the bag. "How bad was it?"

"About three trips to the dumpster's worth, I figure," Thomas said.

"Thomas."

"I missed four out of ten."

Ms. Hall smiled and rubbed her eyes. "Wrong. That's four bags' worth, easy."

Thomas paused in the kitchen door, the bag hooked over his shoulder like Santa Claus. "Hey, you know what I was just thinking?"

"Yes. That you're going to have to forfeit video game time to work on your math homework."

"But this would help me with math! How about I start a service here at the complex, taking out people's trash? You know, like Mrs. Tannen next door? She's older. She'd probably love to have someone take out her trash for say . . . a buck a bag?"

"In your dreams," said Ms. Hall. "A quarter, maybe."

"Still, if I did ten bags a day, seven days a week, I'd have . . ."

Melissa and her mother exchanged a smile. "We're waiting," Melissa said.

"Well, I'd have a ton of money. I could help pay for stuff. You know, electricity and stuff. And gym shoes."

"Thomas, hon. You don't have to help pay for

electricity. I'll find another job. I don't want you worrying, okay?"

"Okay."

Ms. Hall smiled. "Now the gym shoes, that's another story."

Thomas smiled back. "After I take out the trash, I'm going to go make flyers to put under everybody's doors."

An idea, a wonderful, brilliant, way-too-obvious idea was blossoming inside Melissa's head. She forced a hug on Thomas. "Thomas, you are a genius."

"Let go before I croak of woman germs." Thomas yanked himself free.

"Dinner in ten minutes," her mother called as he ran off. She eyed Melissa skeptically. "What was that about?"

"Nothing. Just trying to build up the little toadlet's self-esteem."

"Uh-huh. You're holding out on me, Melissa Sue Hall." She reached for the afternoon paper and opened it to the want ads. "So, hon. How'd things go at school?"

"Not bad, I guess. It's different from Maryland, more mellow. I met some okay kids. And Jenna and Katie were there, so that made it a thousand times better."

"And at Silver Creek?" her mother asked gently, scanning the ads.

"Sharon's going to be interviewed by some girl at the paper."

"Marta Aritas. Cute girl, very gung-ho. I hope Sharon doesn't mind my suggesting that she'd make a good interview. It's just such an inspiring story—"

"I don't think she's exactly thrilled. But that's just Sharon. She's very low-key about stuff like that. Now, *Jenna* would pay to be on the front page."

"So what else happened?"

"I worked on flying changes." Melissa got up to check the macaroni. "When you canter to the cross-over point of a figure eight, the horse switches his lead leg. On Big Red, it's so subtle it's like you're floating on air—"

"You know what I mean, Lissa. Did you tell them you have to quit lessons for a while?"

"Yeah," Melissa said. "It was okay, Mom, really. No big deal."

It was the first time Melissa could remember lying to her mother about anything important. It was so effortless, it surprised her. It scared her a little, too.

"Maybe it won't be for long," her mother said.

"Maybe," Melissa said softly, stirring the pot.

"Melissa, where are you going?" Jenna asked as Melissa climbed onto her bike after school the next day. "This is Sharon's big interview day, have you forgotten? We're supposed to meet over at the restaurant."

"I just have to make one quick stop."

"Let me guess." Katie wagged a finger at her. "You talked your mom into that coat at Mane Street."

"No, I . . . we sort of decided to put that idea on hold."

"What happened to the old get-down-on-your-knees-and-beg?" Jenna asked as she tried, unsuccessfully, to stuff her saxophone case into her backpack.

Melissa shrugged. "I guess I overdid it. She said with talent like mine, I should try out for the school play."

As soon as the words were out of her mouth, Melissa marveled at how easily she was continuing to deceive her friends. She pushed her bike back. Students streamed around them, a laughing, screeching mass of giddy humanity, reveling in the fact that it was three o'clock and they were, once again, temporarily free. "I'll meet you there in a few minutes," Melissa said.

"We could go with you," Katie offered.

"Wherever that is," Jenna added. She nudged Katie. "See? We're being snubbed again. Pretty soon we'll have to bow whenever we're in her magnificent eighth-grade presence."

"Or walk three paces behind her in the halls," Katie added.

"I'm just . . . I've got to get my cousin a present, and if you two go with me, it'll end up taking twice as long. I'm a very focused shopper, you know."

"Fine," Jenna said in mock pain. "Snub away."

"See you there," Melissa called, pedaling off. "Peons."

She maneuvered her way through a gauntlet of guys in the parking lot. They made the usual annoying, obscene, toddler-level guy noises. Who was it, she wondered as she shifted gears and picked up speed, who'd convinced members of the male species to express themselves in grunts and hoots?

As she turned down the newly paved road that was the short-cut to Silver Creek Stables, another, more pressing, question nagged at her. Why was it so easy for her to lie, all of a sudden? She'd lied to her mother. She'd lied to her friends. Why?

She pedaled faster and faster, a rhythmic movement almost like posting. Still, a Schwinn was a poor substitute for a horse. Trees blended to a green blur as she whizzed along, grateful for the bike lane that made traveling this route possible. A curious cow bellowed a greeting as she passed. Soon her nagging question faded to background noise, and all Melissa concentrated on was her goal.

It was very simple—so simple even Thomas could have figured it out—and he had, in a way. Melissa would do chores at Silver Creek in exchange for lessons. Simple.

And the best part was, no one would have to know. She could work in the mornings before school. Her friends would never even know what she was up to. She still wouldn't be able to afford the Autumn Horse Show fee, but she'd come up with an excuse for missing it. A wedding her mother was making her attend. A funeral. Something.

Last night, lying awake while she watched the moon carve designs on her ceiling, she had considered trying to borrow the money from Katie and Jenna and Sharon. But as quickly as the idea had flashed into Melissa's head, it had evaporated. She couldn't do that, couldn't admit to them how tight things had gotten at home. She didn't know why. She just couldn't. And in any case, they weren't exactly rich themselves.

This way was the only way. And if all went well, it would mean she could keep riding.

As she struggled up the long gravel drive that led to the stable, Melissa caught sight of Rose, the owner of Silver Creek. She was wearing a black sweatshirt with a picture of a Thoroughbred silk-screened on the front, a pair of worn jeans, and a Mets baseball cap over her short-cropped gray hair. Angie, the new boarder, was talking to her.

"Melissa, girl! What brings you here?" Rose called as Melissa parked her bike near the office.

As Melissa approached, Angie headed off, shaking her head slightly.

"I hope I'm not interrupting anything," Melissa said.

"Angie, you mean?" Rose shrugged. "I was just telling her she doesn't need to use her crop when her natural aids will do the trick. To which she replied that she is a boarder here, not a student, but thank you very much for the unsolicited advice." She draped her arm around Melissa's shoulder. "I'm sixty-three years old and I still haven't figured out when to keep my mouth shut and mind my own business. Think there's any hope?"

"Knowing you, Rose, I doubt it."

Rose laughed her patented, deep-in-the-belly laugh. "That's why I like you, Melissa. You're brutally honest. A rare quality in today's world."

That's me, Melissa thought. *Brutally honest. Unless, of course, I'm keeping secrets from everyone I know.*

"Come," Rose said. "Escape Route's flirting with a cough. We've got him isolated in the south barn in case he's got an upper respiratory infection. Gary's taking a look-see. We can talk on the way."

Gary Stone, Margaret's husband, was the vet of choice for local horse owners, not to mention an all-around nice guy. During both sessions of camp, he'd give occasional lectures on horse care to the campers.

They started toward the barn, and suddenly Melissa felt her tongue freeze up. Rose was the easiest person in the world to talk to, part affectionate grandmother, part tolerant big sister. And it was a simple enough request. But still. It was one thing to *think* about asking for a job. It was another to actually go through with it.

"You didn't just come here to bask in the glow of my winning personality, now, did you?" Rose chided.

"No."

"That's it, score some points, kid."

"I need . . ." Melissa couldn't seem to say it.

They stepped into the warm, hay-perfumed barn. In the stall at the far end, Gary was examining Escape. "Be right there, Gary," Rose called.

Gary waved and Escape gave them a welcoming whinny. Melissa closed her eyes and breathed in the sweet smells. She couldn't lose this. Couldn't. Even if it meant being embarrassed. Even if it meant taking charity.

"Melissa? Should I fill in the blank? Give me a clue. Animal, vegie, mineral?"

"Um, animal, in a way."

"Could you narrow that down a bit?"

Melissa bit her lip. "I need a job because my mom's getting laid off at the paper and the only way I can keep taking lessons is if you let me like come in the mornings and do chores." The words came out in a furious tumble.

"Darlin'." Rose hugged her. "Is that all? Of course you can have a job. Actually, you're a godsend. Art just asked me the other day if he could go part-time because he's taking some classes at the community college. How about we make it whatever you can squeeze in before school, in exchange for your regular lesson? Sound fair?"

Melissa blinked, trying to let it sink in.

She had a job. She could keep riding.

"Rose," she whispered, "you don't know what this means to me."

"You don't know what this means to *me*. I was going to have to be the one mucking out those stalls."

"One thing, though."

"Already she wants a raise!"

"This is very important. I don't want anyone to

know about this, except the staff. No one is here that early, except maybe you and Claire, when she takes out Wishful Thinking for his morning ride. So it should be easy to keep a secret."

"A secret?" Rose frowned. "But why?" She shook a finger at Melissa. "There's nothing to be embarrassed about, Melissa. Lots of people go through tough times. It just makes you tougher. When my husband and I, rest his soul, were just starting out, there were times when we lived on macaroni and cheese for months."

Melissa smiled ruefully. "You'll never guess what I had for dinner last night."

"Hon, there's no shame in this."

"I know."

"Do you really?"

Melissa didn't answer.

"Besides," Rose said, "you know what Benjamin Franklin said about secrets. *Three may keep a secret, if two of them are dead.*"

"Meaning?"

"Meaning one way or another, secrets have a way of leaking out."

Melissa smiled. "My mom likes quotes, too."

"Your mom's a great lady."

Melissa looked at Rose plaintively. "A secret, okay?"

"Your secret," Rose vowed, "is safe with me, my girl."

"I'll bet Sharon's not coming," Jenna whispered. She and Katie were sitting in a corner booth at McCloud

Nine. The little health food restaurant was having its late afternoon lull, freeing Jenna from her table-bussing duties.

McCloud Nine was a tiny place, just a few tables and three booths. Plants rained from the ceiling, and a blue and white cloud mural covered one wall. Jenna's mother was in the kitchen whipping up her famous tofu hot dogs. Jenna's father, who worked part-time as a math professor at the same college where Katie's parents taught, occasionally helped out at the restaurant, too. His idea of health food was leaving the nuts off a hot fudge sundae, so Jenna's mother tried to keep him as far from the kitchen as possible.

"Sharon will come," Katie said confidently. She gave a discreet nod toward a small table across the room. "Do you think that's the reporter from the *Gazette*?"

At the table, a young woman with wavy dark hair fiddled nervously with a palm-sized tape recorder. Across from her sat an older man with equally long hair, a wispy mustache, and a bulky camera.

"Either that, or they're here to review the food," Jenna whispered. "In which case we're in real trouble, because I'm pretty sure I saw an ant in her salad when I brought her a napkin."

"Jen! Why didn't you say something?"

"Hey, it's protein." She grabbed a pitcher of herbal tea from a stand behind the booth. "I'm going to go spy."

"Behave," Katie warned.

Jenna sauntered over to the reporter. "More tea?"

"No thanks, I'm fine."

"Don't worry," Jenna said. "She'll be here soon. Sharon's always late."

"How did you—"

"The camera, the recorder. It doesn't take a rocket scientist. Besides, I'm a reporter myself."

"Oh, really?"

"I wrote a couple stories for the Silver Creek Middle School *Barker*. That's our school paper. Our mascot's a bulldog, get it? Oh, and I'm also a renowned poet."

"Impressive. I'm Marta Aritas." She extended her hand and Jenna shook it. "And this is Jack Reese."

"Hey," Jenna said. She grabbed an extra chair and straddled it. "So. You want the inside scoop on Sharon?"

"Jenna," Katie called, waving a warning finger.

"I'm just being helpful. I'm a confidential source."

Jack frowned at his tea. "You got anything here with caffeine in it?"

"Sorry. My mom's sort of a purist. Too bad my dad's not here today. He makes killer coffee. Looks just like mud."

Marta retrieved a pen and a notebook. "So you know Sharon. Tell me about her."

"Well, she's really incredible. She was in our tent this summer at camp and at first she was sort of stand-offish. But then she started to open up and now we're really tight. Katie over there, me—Jenna McCloud—" she peered at Marta's notebook, "that's big M, little c, big C—"

"And *loud*," Katie said, joining them.

"Don't mind Katie," Jenna said. "She doesn't understand the way a free press operates. Also, she's a little shy."

"Actually," Katie said, "there's a difference between being shy and knowing when to keep your mouth shut."

"And don't forget to add Melissa Hall," Jenna said. "She and Sharon used to compete against each other. That's us. The Silver Creek Riders."

"You mentioned competing," Marta said, clicking on her tape recorder. "Tell me about this Autumn Horse Show. It's a big deal?"

"The biggest fall show in this region," Jenna said. "We're all entered. It's the first accredited show for Katie and me."

"There are lots of classes and riders coming from all over the area," Katie added. "There will be showmanship classes—that's when you judge the turnout of the horse—you know, his health and grooming and the condition of his tack. Also the skill of his handler."

"And then there are the equitation and performance classes," Jenna said as Marta scribbled away in her notebook.

"Equitation?" Marta asked.

"That's the art of riding, basically, where the rider's judged, not the horse. You might have an equitation over fences class, or one on the flat— that's without fences. Now, with performance classes, it's the *horse's* performance that's being judged. That would be a class like hunter under saddle—that's on the flat. Or like the hunter jumping class I'm entered in."

"Whoa. Slow down. I can't write that fast."

"You have a tape recorder," Jenna pointed out.

"I like to take notes, just in case the batteries wear out." Marta shook her head. "This jumping class—is that where you race around over jumps and the fastest horse wins?"

"No, that's a jumper class. In a hunter class, style's the important thing," Jenna explained. "The judge is looking at *how* the horse jumps and how he moves around the course. In a jumper event, fences tend to be higher, and the fastest clear round wins."

"Will Sharon be in any of those?"

"No," Katie said. "She used to do a lot of jumping, but her legs aren't strong enough yet."

"Too bad," Jack said. "It'd make for better pictures."

"And how do you think Sharon will do in her classes?" Marta asked.

"Anyone want my potato chips?" Jack interrupted. "They don't have any salt. I mean, what's the point of potato chips without salt?"

"Well," Jenna said, grabbing a handful of chips, "Sharon's an incredibly gifted rider. I mean, she was one of the top riders in New England before her accident. Even now, with her braces, she's made a lot of progress. I think she'll do great. I wouldn't be surprised if she took first in her class."

"Still," Katie added, "she's a much different rider now—"

"Different how?" Marta asked.

Katie hesitated. "I just mean, I don't think we should put any more pressure on Sharon than is already there. This is her very first show in a long time—"

"There's Melissa," Jenna said, pointing. Melissa was outside the restaurant, locking her bike to a nearby rack.

"That's Hall, big H—"

"Little *all*, yeah," Marta said.

Melissa opened the door, blasting the restaurant with the chill afternoon air. "Hey," she said, grinning. "Where's Sharon?"

"Late, as usual," Jenna said.

"Did you get your aunt something?" Katie asked.

"My—oh. No, couldn't find anything. Guess I should have dragged you peons along, after all."

"Melissa, I'm Marta Aritas, and this is Jack Reese. I intern at the paper. Your mom's really been an inspiration to me."

At the mention of her mother, Melissa's smile faded. "I'll be sure to tell her that." She took a step back. "I'm going to go grab a booth. You two coming?"

"In a minute," Jenna said. "I'm being a confidential source."

"Potato chip?" Jack asked. Melissa shook her head.

"It's lousy, the way the paper's treating her," Marta

continued. "I mean, she's a great reporter—"

"Treating her how?" Katie asked curiously.

"Oh—" Melissa shrugged. "You know. The way all papers treat their staff—"

"Like roach dung," Jack volunteered.

"Exactly," Melissa agreed quickly.

Sharon appeared at the door, releasing a second wave of frigid air. "Well, I see the gang's all here," she said grimly.

Jenna watched as Marta and Jack smiled at Sharon. In perfect unison, their eyes dropped down to her braces. She must get so tired of that, Jenna thought. Good thing Sharon was tough enough to handle it.

"What have you told them, you three?" Sharon demanded.

"Just your innermost secrets," Jenna volunteered.

"I already confessed to Marta that I don't have any."

"We improvised." Jenna wiggled her brows. "Juicy stuff, really hot."

"Come on," Melissa urged. "Let's give them some privacy."

"If I wanted privacy, would I be talking to a reporter?" Sharon asked as she sat next to Marta. "Come to think of it, why *am* I talking to you?"

"You felt sorry for me," Marta replied.

Katie yanked on Jenna's shirt collar. "Jenna . . ."

Reluctantly, Jenna stood. Melissa was already camped out in a booth on the other side of the restaurant. "Let me know if you need anything," Jenna said.

Jack frowned. "Caffeine, salt and sugar would be nice," he said.

"Let's get this over with," Sharon said. "Before I change my mind."

4

"And now a blast from the past from the Monkees!"

Sharon slammed down the alarm button on her clock radio. Sean had been fiddling with the stations again, the cretin, just to annoy her.

She liked to wake up to classical, something soothing that didn't involve amplifiers. Later, when she was more awake, she switched to the alternative rock station in Pooleville. But first thing in the morning . . .

She squinted at the green numbers on her clock. Four A.M. Way, way too first thing in the morning.

Her eyes drifted shut.

Then she remembered the interview yesterday afternoon.

She sat up, suddenly alert. The words came back to her. Marta's insistent questioning, Sharon's hesitant responses.

Do you think you'll ever be the champion you used to be, Sharon?

Well, you know, it's hard to say. I have to believe I might be, because it gives me something to shoot for. But I also have to accept that I can live with less. And

I can. I started to realize that at camp this summer.
And to appreciate riding for the sheer fun of riding.
It's not just about competition.

Really it isn't.

So your goals for the horse show are—?

Just to do as well as I can. A show should be
about competing against yourself. Not about seeing
who takes home the most blues. It's a way to gauge
your progress.

*I understand you won't be entered in any jumping
classes.*

Well, no. I'm not ready for that. My legs aren't
strong enough. I'll just be in a walk/trot class. Pretty
basic stuff. *Really* basic, actually.

And you're okay with that?

Sure I am. The important thing is to do as well as
you can, no matter what your level. Yeah, sure, I'm
okay with that.

*Still, it'll be hard, watching other competitors jump.
I'm sure it'll bring back memories of riding with your
own horse . . . what was her name?*

Cassidy. And I don't need to watch other horses
to do that. I remember her every day. I'll always
remember her. She was the best.

Um, I think the interview's over now, okay?

• • •

Last night Sharon had dreamed about Cass. Not the old, scary nightmare, the one she'd had so often, even at camp. Just a wonderful dream where they'd flown over every obstacle in their path, tooling around Miller Falls and Pooleville like Cass was a four-legged pogo stick.

Well, that wasn't what this show was about. It was about walking and trotting. Period. End of story.

She'd told Marta that she didn't care about the rest, about the jumping and the ribbons and the trophies. And this morning Sharon was going to go for a little ride, just to make sure she'd been telling Marta the truth.

Sharon's father, who for some insane reason felt compelled to get up early and jog before heading off to work, had promised to drive her to the stables. She'd called Claire, who always took Wishful Thinking out for a dawn trail ride, and had gotten the okay to come by.

"Are you sure you want to do this?" Sharon's father asked when she made her way blearily to the kitchen.

"No," Sharon answered. "Let's go."

Melissa's alarm buzzed at exactly four-thirty, but she was already up and showered by then. Her books were in a neat pile, her school clothes in another. Organization, she'd decided, was going to be the trick to making this job work.

Her mom was going to drive her to the stable—

she'd insisted there was no way Melissa was riding her bike there before it was light outside. Melissa would put her bike in the back of their station wagon, then, after her work at the stable was done, she would change her clothes and pedal the short way to school. The only thing that worried her was wandering the halls the rest of the day, reeking of eau de horse.

To her pile of clothes, Melissa added a bottle of deodorant. Good thing she had P.E. second period. She could shower then.

Her mother was in the kitchen, already dressed, perusing, as usual, the want ads. A pot of oatmeal sat on the stove.

"Hot, nutritious breakfast," her mother said. "Important for us working women."

"Thanks, Mom. But you didn't have to."

"It's the least I can do." The guilt in her voice made Melissa nervous.

"Mom, I love being at the stables, you know that. This is going to be fun."

"I'm worried about your schoolwork, Lissa. You're going to be exhausted."

"I'll get used to it. Besides, you know me. I'm an early riser, anyway." Melissa spooned some oatmeal into a bowl and added some brown sugar. "You wouldn't believe how great the stable is first thing in the morning. It's so peaceful. And the horses are so excited to see you. They're like little kids, all hyped up. It's so cute."

Her mother smiled. "I'm glad you can keep riding,

Lissa. I'm sorry about the show, though."

"There'll be other shows. And I can help Jenna and Katie and Sharon. It'll almost be the same thing."

"I imagine they've been very supportive about all this," her mother said, sipping at her coffee. "It's nice to have friends to talk to when things get complicated."

Melissa reached for the front page section and unfolded it. "Mm-hmm," she murmured.

Silence fell. The wall clock ticked too loudly.

"Lissa, you didn't tell them, did you?"

Melissa put down the paper and shoved her bowl aside. "It's my business what I tell and don't tell my friends, Mom. If I want it to be a secret, that's my right, isn't it?" Her sharp tone surprised her.

"Of course it is."

"So can we just drop this?"

"Friends are there for listening, Melissa."

Melissa shoved back her chair. It scraped on the linoleum, leaving a black trail. "I'm going to go get my stuff. I'll meet you in the car."

"Look. I understand if you're angry at me. You feel like I let you down, and maybe I did. But don't take it out on yourself, okay? Secrets are like splinters. They have this way of festering until they come out."

"I am not angry at you," Melissa said firmly. "And I certainly am not festering. I am just anxious to go start my new job, okay?"

"Okay. You're sure you want to do this?"

"Yes. Now let's go."

•   •   •

Claire was already waiting for Sharon in the indoor ring. She was riding Wishful Thinking, a big, gorgeous black mare who had been Claire's mount when she was younger.

Wish was a sensitive, highly trained horse. Although she was semi-retired, she carried herself with the brash, proud bearing of the champion she was, the horse that had taken Claire all the way to the finals for the U.S. Olympic team.

She was Sharon's dream horse. A perfect mount, in the old days. A recipe for disaster these days.

"I thought you were hitting the trails," Sharon said, tossing aside her down jacket and scarf. Sharon much preferred riding outside, but there were days— like this one—when an indoor ring was an absolute necessity.

"Most mornings. Too cold today."

"For Wish or for you?"

Claire grinned at her, then executed a half-pass, a graceful dressage movement where the horse moves half-forward, half-sideways, crossing his legs under him. In Claire's capable hands, she and Wishful Thinking might as well have been communicating telepathically. They made a beautiful pair, Claire with her short dark curly hair and intense blue eyes and Wish, with her sleek sable coat. Graceful and devoted athletes, the two of them. Sometimes a horse and rider just seemed meant for each other.

Claire was the rider Sharon could have been. Sometimes that made their teacher-student relationship a little edgy, but it also gave them a unique bond of understanding. They'd first met in a circumstance Sharon would have liked to forget, when Claire was a volunteer teacher at a local equestrian rehabilitation center called PET, the Program for Equestrian Therapy. Sharon had attended a few sessions, then dropped out. She was too good a rider, even after her accident, to be condemned to circling a ring on a mount so sleepy and gentle it might as well have been stuffed.

Claire walked Wishful Thinking over. "You know," she said, "you look like warmed-over gruel this early in the morning, Sharon."

Sharon stroked Wish's flank. "I'm going to ignore that remark, since you're doing me a favor here."

"What's this all about, anyway? It's a little early for pre-show jitters. Especially for an old war horse like you." Claire cocked her head. "This wouldn't have anything to do with that interview yesterday, would it?"

"Could be," Sharon hedged. "That reporter kept asking how I thought I'd do and what would it be like to go back in the ring competitively, and I guess it got me to thinking."

"So this is a sort of practice run. To see how you're going to do?"

Sharon busied herself with removing a piece of hay from Wish's mane. The truth was, it was a practice run to see how completely humiliated she was going to feel. But there was no point in getting into that with

Claire. She'd just give her some song-and-dance about Sharon doing the best she could.

"I guess I should go warm up Blooper," Sharon said. She would be riding the sweet-natured bay in the show.

"Why would you do that, when I've got Wish primed for action?" Claire dismounted and passed the reins and her hard hat to Sharon.

"But—"

"We'll just take him through the basics of your class. Nothing you can't handle in your sleep."

"Good thing, since as it happens, I *am* asleep."

Sharon managed to mount Wishful Thinking on her second try. Not bad, she thought with grim determination, given that it sometimes took a half-dozen tries before she was up in the saddle. Her left leg was her weakest, and mounting always put a huge strain on her unreliable muscles and the bones that had been badly crushed in the accident.

"Now," Claire said, stepping to the center of the arena. "Just imagine I'm your judge. And there are several other competitors in the ring with you."

"And hundreds of people in the stands watching."

Claire gave her a dubious smile. "Come on. This is a flat class. Walk/trot, piece of cake. You're more than ready to handle it. And it's not like you haven't performed before a crowd before."

"Yeah, I know," Sharon said. Wishful Thinking tossed her head and shifted beneath Sharon restlessly.

"I know it's been a long time since you've competed,

Sharon," Claire said gently. "But you'll do fine, more than fine. I wouldn't even be surprised if you walked away with a ribbon."

"Walked, is right."

"There will be other competitions. You'll be jumping someday soon."

Sharon hesitated. How could she explain the truth to Claire, that this wasn't just the usual case of show jitters? This was about being seen by all the people who'd known her as the other Sharon, the gifted rider. It was about the horrible feeling of being pitied.

On the ground, at least, she could handle it. She'd gotten used to the stares and averted gazes at school. And to her surprise, she'd noticed that kids were beginning to seem more accepting of her disability. She was still Sharon, that girl with braces, but she was also Sharon, the soprano soloist in glee club, and Sharon, the one who cracked that disgusting joke during the worm dissection in science class.

Camp had been the same way, especially with the support and friendship of Katie and Melissa and Jenna. But the show would be different. The show would be full of people she'd competed against, people who'd heard of her but didn't necessarily know her well. All of them whispering and tut-tutting in the stands.

Even Katie, the newest rider of the four friends, would be competing in a more difficult class. And Sharon would have to watch Melissa, Melissa whom she'd once competed against and beaten, sailing over oxers and gates, while Sharon could barely manage to mount her horse without humiliating herself.

"Ready?" Claire asked.

"As a comatose person can be."

"All right then. The walk/trot class has just been announced. You've got your new riding clothes on. You've got your number—let's say, eleven—a nice all-around number, if I do say so myself. Blooper has been groomed to a glorious shine. His hooves are gleaming. His mane and tail are perfectly braided. You guys are looking sharp."

Sharon pretended to snore.

"Okay, okay. I was just setting the mood." Claire cleared her throat. "Riders—or I guess I should say rider—begin with a counterclockwise walk."

Sharon nudged Wishful Thinking into a walk.

"Watch your left heel position, Sharon."

Sharon gritted her teeth. It was hard to keep her heel down. Her Achilles' tendon had been partially severed in the accident, and it hurt like crazy when she tried to bend her foot too far.

"Let's see a sitting trot, starting at B," Claire instructed.

Halfway down the ring, Sharon legged Wishful Thinking into a trot. She had a bouncier gait than Blooper, and Sharon sat it with difficulty.

"Let's keep those lower legs still," Claire called. "And a nice steady contact on the reins."

"Since when do judges offer helpful hints to the competitors?" Sharon called back.

"So I'm biased. Also, watch the puppy paws."

Sharon glanced down. Claire was right. Her wrists were bent. It was the kind of simple mistake she never would have made in the old days. But in the old days, she hadn't had so much to think about. Sometime she got that same overwhelmed feeling she used to have when she'd just started riding lessons. She felt like a three-year-old trying to drive an eighteen-wheeler.

"Figure eight at a rising trot," Claire instructed.

Sharon gritted her teeth. Posting gave her more trouble than anything else. She began rising on the left diagonal as she circled to the right, but when she reached the X at the center of the ring and sat for two beats, her left leg slipped out of the stirrup. Wish tried to surge forward, but Sharon kept her trot even, and, after two tries, managed to catch her stirrup and complete her figure eight.

"Nice recovery," Claire called.

Nice recovery. Exactly. That's just what all those people in the stands would be saying. Nice recovery, under the circumstances.

She was embarrassed already.

"Okay, Sharon, why don't you bring her back down to a walk, clockwise?" Claire called. "She's a handful, huh? But that's why I wanted you to ride her this morning. If you can do this well on Wish, you'll sail through your class on old Bloop."

She knew Claire was just trying to be nice. One good thing, at least—no one else had witnessed Sharon's first attempt to return to the show ring.

Behind her, Sharon heard the ring door open. Who

would be coming here this time of day? It had to be Rose.

Sharon glanced over her shoulder.

It wasn't Rose. It was Melissa. And she looked almost as surprised to see Sharon as Sharon was to see her.

5

"Sharon! What are you doing here at this hour?" Melissa cried.

Sharon reined Wishful Thinking to a halt. "You know what an early riser I am."

"Yeah, right. It took a stick of dynamite to get you out of your cot at camp."

"Well . . ." Sharon hesitated. "I guess after that interview yesterday, I was kind of wound up about the show. Claire was just running me through some stuff."

"And you feel better now, right?" Claire prompted.

"Much," Sharon said, but something in her voice told Melissa she wasn't quite telling the whole truth and nothing but.

"Although I have to admit that old Blooper's starting to look better and better as a mount," Sharon added. She began to carefully dismount. "So how about you?"

Melissa caught Claire's eye. Rose had probably told Claire that Melissa was going to be working at the stable. The question was, had Claire told Sharon?

"You know what an early riser I am," Melissa

repeated, buying time. At least in her case, it was actually true.

"Here, Sharon," Claire said, taking Wishful Thinking's reins. "I'll walk him out. You probably need to get going, anyway."

Sharon checked her watch. "Oh, man, I've got to hurry. The bus goes by here in eight minutes." She grabbed her jacket and scarf and handed Claire the hard hat she was wearing. "Thanks again, Claire."

"Any time. You looked fine, Sharon. Really."

Sharon gave a half-smile, half-grimace. "So," she said, joining Melissa at the door. "Really. How come you're here at this hour? This isn't exactly on the way to school for you."

They headed out into the faint dawn light. Their breath hung in the air in frosted balloons. "I left my math homework in my locker," Melissa said.

"So how are you getting to school?" Sharon asked, wrapping her scarf in loose loops around her neck.

Melissa hesitated. "My mom dropped me off with my bike."

"She didn't wait for you?"

"Well, see, she was late to a meeting. And I have to stay after school late for a . . . a meeting, too, so I knew I'd need my bike to get home."

"What meeting?"

"Um, I'm thinking about joining . . . the computer club."

"Sounds like fun, I guess. In a technological sort of way. Me, riding's all the hobby I can handle." Sharon checked her watch again. "I gotta run." She smiled self-deprecatingly. "Or at least walk fast."

Melissa sighed with relief as Sharon started down the drive. She had never been so glad to say goodbye to a good friend. "Hey, when does that article come out?" she called.

"Soon. A day or two, I think. Don't remind me."

Sharon crunched down the drive. Melissa watched her slow, labored walk and felt a wave of affection and respect for her friend. Sharon was so strong. It had to be tough, dealing with the stares and pity of strangers, and yet she handled it with such grace and good humor.

So why, a nagging voice that sounded way too much like her mother demanded, was Melissa handling her own problems so badly? Why all the secrets and evasions?

Because, she told herself, switching on the light in the tack room, it was no one's business what her family's financial situation was. That was all. Besides, if she told people, they'd just feel sorry for her.

She began methodically straightening bits and bridles. She'd have to work quickly if she was going to hay the horses and muck out their stalls. Fortunately, she didn't have to do the whole place herself. Gordy, one of the stablehands, would be here in another forty-five minutes. Rose had told her he would finish up whatever Melissa couldn't get to.

Still, she wanted to do a thorough job. She

decided to start with the horses who required dietary supplements. Escape Route would need a warm bran mash this morning, too. Melissa was ticking off a list of chores in her mind when she noticed Gary and Margaret Stone drive up.

"Melissa," Margaret said cheerfully as she climbed out of Gary's truck. "Rose told me you were going to be helping out. She's thrilled to have you, by the way."

"Did she also tell you . . . you know, not to mention it?"

"My lips are sealed," Margaret said. "As a matter of fact, I'm going to run to the office before they freeze shut permanently." She gave Gary a quick kiss. "See you tonight."

"I'm just going to make a quick check on Escape Route before I head to the clinic," Gary explained to Melissa as he headed toward the south barn.

Fifteen minutes later, when Melissa began tossing hay in the racks, she was surprised to find Gary with AB, the horse that Angie was boarding.

"I thought you said you were here to see Escape," Melissa said, peering over the stall door.

"I was. He's doing fine, by the way. But on my way out, I thought I'd wander through the stable and say hello to the gang. I love it in the morning, you know?"

Melissa nodded. "It's so peaceful."

"Anyway, I happened to notice a little abrasion near this guy's right eye. Probably hit a branch out on the trail."

AB stood very still as Gary examined the small cut. His movements were so gentle and slow that AB didn't seem the least bit threatened. Gary looked like your basic big brother—jean jacket, baseball cap, faded flannel shirt—but he was the most respected equine vet in the area. People brought their horses from hundreds of miles away to get his opinion on difficult cases.

"It's amazing, the way they let you help them, isn't it?" Melissa marveled. "I mean, it's almost like they know you're trying to help."

"I like to think they do," Gary said. "Course this guy makes it easy, he's so mellow. You know his owner?"

"I just met her the other day. Angie. She seems nice."

"I'll have Rose tell her she may want to have her own vet check that out, although it's just a minor cut. She's not my client, and since she's a boarder here, I can't even put antibiotic on without her permission." He picked up his battered bag and smiled at Melissa. "You know, when I was in high school, I helped out at a farm like you're doing, mornings and most afternoons. My dad hurt his back in a construction accident and he was laid up for almost two years. My mom was a secretary, but we didn't have a lot of money."

Melissa felt a lecture coming on. Rose had obviously told Margaret about Melissa's problems, and Margaret had obviously told Gary. So much for keeping secrets.

"Well," Melissa said, turning to go. "I've got a lot of hungry mouths to feed—"

"I was so mad about having to work that way," Gary

continued, stroking the palomino's honey-gold neck. "See, I was on the basketball team—center, mostly— and I had to miss so many practices they kicked me off the team."

Melissa checked her watch.

"You're in a hurry." Gary smiled knowingly. "You want me to skip to the moral of the story?"

Melissa smiled back, in spite of herself. "If you wouldn't mind."

"The moral of the story is that when I look back, I don't remember the games I missed. Much, anyway. But I do remember those mornings in the barn, feeding the horses, milking the cows. The way those animals got so they knew me and needed me. I think that's when I decided to become a vet." He gave an apologetic shrug. "So. Pretty lame story, huh? Jeez. My dad used to do this. Don't you just hate it when the elderly try to pass on their wisdom to unsuspecting victims?"

"Gary," Melissa chided, "you're not elderly."

Gary beamed. "Thanks, Melissa—"

She turned, then added over her shoulder. "I mean, you're *old*, sure. But I'm sure you've got a few good years before the nursing home."

The sound of his laughter echoed on the high wooden rafters as Melissa began working her way down the stalls. Each horse had a different way of greeting her, as delicate and unique as the too-early snowflakes visible through the window over the stable doors.

With Blooper, not a morning-lover, it was a sloppy

headnudge and a deep-in-the-throat whicker, his eyes half-closed in drowsy indifference.

With Say-So, a bay gelding, it was the grumbled greeting of an older gent with a lot on his mind—a whuffle, an impatient, stomped hoof.

Big Red, the chestnut gelding with white stockings, was all exuberant affection, nudging and nuzzling for the possible carrot or sugar cube, whinnying hello, ears pricked, whole body on alert.

The minutes passed too quickly. Melissa consulted her watch again. She was going to be late to first period. She should be hurrying, but instead she lingered in each stall. And with every new greeting, each gentle moment of affection, Melissa's worries faded a little more. These four-footed friends were her life, and one way or another they always would be.

Maybe Gary had a point. As tired as she was, as late as she was going to be, she was beginning to realize that she'd probably pay Rose for the chance to do this job.

Melissa was struggling to open her locker—it never failed to jam when she was in a hurry—when she heard Jenna's voice cutting through the post-first period traffic congestion in the hall.

"Melissa!" Jenna cried, rushing up to her with Katie close behind, "where were you this morning? We were supposed to meet by Katie's locker."

"I . . . overslept," Melissa said quickly. Again she felt that lie-induced panic. What if Sharon mentioned that she'd seen Melissa at the stable? "And then," she added quickly, just in case, "I had to go by the stable to pick up my math book."

"That would explain the piece of hay stuck to your sweater," Katie said, plucking it off Melissa's back.

Whoops. She was going to have to remember to check for telltale signs like that. She wondered if she smelled like the stables. She'd laid on the deodorant pretty thick, just to be on the safe side.

"Gotta go," Melissa said. "I was already late to first period and Coach Hollis will fry me if I'm late for P.E. See you at lunch?"

"You sure you're okay, Melissa?" Katie asked, a look of concern in her round, dark eyes. "You seem sort of frazzled."

"Maybe she's up to something," Jenna whispered to Katie. "Could be she's having some kind of secret rendezvous like you were at camp with Matt."

"I was rendezvousing with his horse," Katie reminded her. During the second session of camp, she'd befriended Romance, a beautiful chestnut mare. Later, she'd befriended his very cute owner as well.

"Sorry, no rendezvous. I lead an amazingly dull life," Melissa said. "See you at lunch."

She flowed into the rush of students before Katie and Jenna could grill her anymore. Halfway to the gym, she noticed Angie talking to a tall blond guy with a basketball under one arm. Melissa instinctively veered across the hall—there was no point in talking

to anyone else from the stable today—but it was too
late.

"Hi! Melissa, right?" Angie said, waving. Melissa
slowed, dodged an eighth-grade couple making out,
and made her way over to Angie's locker.

"Melissa, this is Dave, Dave, Melissa."

"Hey," he said, grinning. "Nice to meet you."

There was an awkward pause. Melissa hated
awkward pauses. "I was just talking to Gary Stone
about AB," she said to fill the empty space. Instantly
she regretted opening her mouth.

"When did you see Gary?" Angie asked, frowning.

"I had to go by the stable to pick up my math
book." The third time today she'd used that bogus
story. "Gary happened to notice that cut near AB's
right eye. He said you might want to have someone
take a look at it, just to be on the safe side, but he
thought it was no big deal."

"It *was* no big deal," Angie said curtly. "And what
right does Gary Stone have to be snooping around my
horse without my permission?"

"He was there to look at another horse, is all. He
wasn't snooping."

"It's nothing, anyway," Angie said with a dismissive
gesture. "AB ran into a branch over by the creek
yesterday, the idiot. He's not the most observant
animal I've ever known."

"Gary said it was probably something like that."
Melissa hesitated. "Really, he was just trying to be
helpful, Angie."

Angie smiled coolly. "I'm just sort of protective when it comes to my horse. And you all seem, well, a little nosy over there at Silver Creek, if you don't mind my saying so. I *am* just a boarder. Yesterday that Rose woman was bugging me about using my crop too much. I mean, who is she to be telling me how to ride?"

"Rose is really great, though," Melissa said. "You'll love her once you get to know her."

"I'm sure you're right," Angie said with another veiled smile. "Well, it was nice seeing you again, Melissa. I'll probably run into you around the stable."

Something about that girl didn't sit quite right, Melissa thought as Angie and Dave headed off in the opposite direction. Although it could be she wasn't being entirely fair. Was she was feeling resentful because Angie could afford her very own horse while Melissa had to work just to be able to afford lessons? Maybe so.

Still, as Melissa dashed toward gym class, she was surprised to realize that she was already thinking about work tomorrow. If she got up a half hour earlier and planned her schedule more efficiently, she'd have even more time to spend with the horses.

Already, she couldn't wait to get back to work.

6

"Hot off the presses." Jenna dropped a newspaper onto Katie's lunch tray.

"The article about Sharon?" Katie asked, setting aside her gray hamburger.

Jenna nodded and settled into a chair. "Burgers any good?"

"The lunch ladies have outdone themselves. How do you suppose they form dryer lint into patties?"

Katie scanned the front page. A boxed story at the bottom caught her eye.

SILVER CREEK STABLES RIDER
BACK IN THE SADDLE AGAIN
*Triumphs over Tragedy as She Heads for Victory
in the Ring*

"It's really a great article," Jenna said, grabbing Katie's fruit cup. "That Marta girl laid it on thick. Lots of stuff about Sharon's inner strength and tireless courage. All true, of course, but Sharon's going to die. Oh, and according to Marta, Sharon has—let me see if I've got this straight now—'a tumbling red mane like volcanic overflow.' "

Katie grinned. "Apparently she has a 'sweet inner charm masked by a dry wit,' too."

"Who'd have guessed it?" Jenna laughed. "It must be true, though. After all, it's in the paper."

"Where'd you get this, anyway?"

"Goober let me have it." Mr. Guberstein was the vice-principal of Silver Creek Middle School. Out of earshot, he was simply "Goober."

"When did you see Goober?"

"When I was in the hall without a pass this morning. We made a deal. I promised not to do it again, he gave me the front section of the paper. I tried for the sports, but he said I could only have that if I promised he wouldn't see me in his office all year long. It seemed like too high a price."

Katie scanned the article more carefully while Jenna began, for some bizarre reason, systematically dismantling Katie's lunch tray.

It was a very nice piece, Katie decided as she read. Sharon would cringe at the florid parts, but Marta had managed to give a real sense of what it had been like to recover from a devastating accident.

"What are you doing to my food?" Katie asked, glancing up from the article.

"I'm making a jump course. Your fruit cup's a gate. The plate of fries is a cross rail. Can I have your burger?"

"No."

"Too bad. I was going to use the lettuce for a brush jump."

"Did you read this part?" Katie asked. She began reading:

After her accident, Finnerty briefly attended the local hippotherapy program that uses horseback riding to improve the motor and mental skills of disabled individuals. It was at PET, or the Program for Equestrian Therapy, that Finnerty met Claire Donovan, a PET volunteer who is also the head instructor at Silver Creek Stables. PET, Donovan explained, works with clients who have many different kinds of disabilities—cerebral palsy, spina bifida, paralysis. Even the learning or emotionally disabled can benefit from the program, with its emphasis on developing self-confidence and improving motor skills.

"Although she wasn't with the PET program long," Donovan said, "Sharon was an excellent role model for the other students."

"I just didn't feel I belonged there," Finnerty said when asked why she left PET, eventually opting for a summer camp experience at Silver Creek. "It was sort of a reminder of my accident. Whereas camp, as hard as it was, was a way of saying, yes, I'm back to riding again."

Katie looked up at Jenna. "Did Sharon ever talk to you about that program at all?"

"She just said she wasn't there very long." Jenna

ılk carton to the center of the table. "Water
explained.

won't be any water jumps on your course."
"True." Jenna moved it a few inches, then paced
off strides, walking her index finger and middle finger
through the course. "Let's make it an in-and-out."

When Katie came to the last paragraph of Marta's
article, she frowned. "I don't know about this ending,"
she said doubtfully.

> When asked to assess her chances for a ribbon
> in the upcoming Autumn Horse Show, Finnerty was
> characteristically understated.
>
> "I just want to do as well as I can," she said. "And
> remember how great it is to be riding again. I won
> plenty of medals on Cassidy. That part of my life is
> over now."
>
> But one look at the determination in Finnerty's
> eyes, and it's obvious she still has all the makings
> of a champion. And if she walks away with a blue
> ribbon in the show, none of her many admirers will
> be at all surprised.

"Do you think that's me?" Jenna asked hopefully.
" 'One of her many admirers'? Marta did ask me what
I thought of Sharon's chances."

"Unfortunately, you answered her." Katie set the
paper aside.

Jenna finger-jumped over the fries. "What do you
mean, unfortunately?" she asked.

"I just think Sharon already feels enough pressure," Katie said. "She doesn't need some news article putting even more on her."

"Everybody feels pressure." Jenna shrugged. "It's part of competing."

"But not the same way Sharon does. This is her first show since the accident. Lots of people are going to be watching her, people who don't know her like we do. People who remember the old Sharon, the girl who won the Classic and took home all those trophies over the years."

Jenna cupped her chin in her hand. "Something else just occurred to me," she said thoughtfully. "I've been sitting here, worrying about whether or not I should have entered that hunter jumping class. I know Claire and Margaret say I'm ready, but still . . . I keep thinking I could go out there and land on my butt and suffer, you know, maximum humiliation."

"Like Matt," Katie said. "He was afraid he wouldn't measure up to his big brother's rep as a rider."

"I was just thinking maybe Sharon's not so much worried about that kind of thing. Maybe she's worried about being in this show at all. I mean, she's only entered in walk/trot, Katie. That's it. You, me, Melissa—we're all entered in more difficult classes."

"Poor Sharon. I wish there were something we could say. But it's probably best if we don't bring it up. It'd just feel like more pressure." Katie grabbed her milk and took a sip.

"Don't drink all that in-and-out," Jenna chided. "I'm thirsty."

"You could try buying your own jump." Katie sighed. "I feel sort of guilty about this show. I don't feel quite as pressured this time, not like the rest of you. Maybe it's because I have my first show under my belt. And I know I'm not in any danger of walking away with the championship or anything."

"Or maybe it's because when you helped Matt you sort of worked through some of that stuff yourself," Jenna suggested. "Now maybe you can keep me sane."

"Way too late for that," Katie joked, but when she saw her best friend's anxious expression, she softened. "We'll all keep each other sane. Remember what Sharon and Melissa kept telling us last summer during the camp show. It's supposed to be *fun*."

"And it was, too," Jenna agreed. "Hey," she said, glancing around the teeming cafeteria, "where is Melissa, anyhow?

"She said she fell asleep early last night before she'd finished her English homework, so she's in the library doing it now."

"Sure she's not snubbing us again?"

"You know," Katie mused, "she has seemed a little distracted lately."

Jenna shrugged. "New school, the show. That's all, probably."

"Probably." Katie fingered her now-cold burger. "You think we'll all stay as close as we were this summer?"

"Well, let's see. We ate together, showered together, slept a couple feet apart together, and pretty much rode together. It'd be hard to top that for togetherness. But yeah, I think we'll be okay."

"It's just that with Sharon going to a different school, and Melissa and Sharon in eighth grade, and you and me in seventh . . ."

"Hey, I have an idea," Jenna said, grabbing Katie's milk.

"It was bound to happen eventually."

"Sarcasm aside," Jenna said, "do you want to hear it or not?"

"This wouldn't be anything like your last big idea? You know, the 'let's-cheer-up-Melissa-by-writing-fake-love-letters' idea that worked out so well?"

"Actually, it's much simpler. I was just going to suggest we have a sleepover. We haven't done that sort of thing in ages."

"I'm stunned to admit this, but that is actually a great idea," Katie said. "We could do the whole nine yards—popcorn, sleeping bags, rent some movies—"

"How about tomorrow night, since we've got lessons Saturday?"

Katie nodded with satisfaction. It would give them all a chance to get their bearings and reconnect. It was important that the Silver Creek Riders stay together. There would be disruptions this year, changes they couldn't predict. But that didn't mean the bonds they'd forged that summer had to change, too.

"Katie?"

Katie was jarred from her thoughts. "Yeah?"

"Can I borrow your lemon meringue pie?" Jenna asked. "I'm short an oxer."

All the horses had been fed. The automatic waterers were checked and cleaned. Every stall had been mucked out.

Melissa stood in the tack room, admiring her handiwork there. She'd arranged the bits according to their frequency of use. Until now, they'd always been stored according to some longstanding habit of Rose's. But this was much more functional. Next time, she'd tackle the challenging wall of bridles. If there was time, she'd work out a better arrangement for the saddle pads and blankets, too.

Melissa checked her watch. By arriving a half-hour earlier, she'd accomplished far more. Rose had already cautioned her about doing too much. Leave something for Gordy to do, she'd chided. But Melissa liked the feeling of working hard, of leaving the stable pristine and well-ordered.

Besides, the more time she spent here, the better. What had been a necessity, a way to insure she could keep riding, had become a reward in itself.

There were down sides to this new job, of course. For one thing, she walked around in a state of near zombiehood much of the time. Last night she'd crashed into bed at eight-thirty—*eight-thirty!* And while her school work hadn't suffered—Melissa was far too dedicated a student for that—she hadn't triple-checked her math homework this week, and her essay on the three branches of government for social studies had only netted her an A-minus.

Still, all things considered, she had to admit that having to take this job was probably the best/worst thing that had ever happened to her.

Melissa made her way down the concrete aisle one more time, saying a last goodbye to each of the horses. Gordy would put them out in the west paddock when he arrived.

She paused in the stable doorway. Angie was out in the largest training ring, taking AB over a small jump course Claire had set up for her classes tomorrow. It was much warmer this morning, almost Indian summer warm. A couple of other boarders had shown up for a quick early-morning ride, too, but they were out on the trails.

As Melissa left the barn, Mischief, Silver Creek's resident goat mascot, ran over and butted her thigh hopefully. "Not exactly subtle, are you?" she said, slipping him the last nub of carrot in her jacket.

Mischief practically inhaled the carrot, then gave a dismissive bleat and trotted off like he owned the place—which, in a way, he did. Everyone, horses included, gave the feisty goat the right-of-way.

Melissa leaned against the rough wooden barn, just slightly warmed by the pale pink sunlight. This, *this* was happiness. She was tired to the bone, but tomorrow, because of all her hard work, she could ride again.

In the training ring, Angie was muscling AB over the jump course, cursing loudly every time the palomino failed to respond. It was a simple enough course—a couple of low verticals, an oxer, a brush jump, but she was having a tough time keeping AB's strides smooth and even. Although she was a couple of years older than Melissa, it was obvious she didn't have as much experience jumping.

"Line him up straight," Melissa murmured as she watched Angie approach the last vertical at too sharp an angle. AB struggled over, his left rear hoof just grazing the fence.

Melissa wondered if she should offer Angie some pointers on jumping. But, recalling her conversation at school with Angie about how nosy everyone at Silver Creek had been, she decided against it.

She checked her watch. She was going to be late to first period again, unless she could find a pair of supersonic rockets to strap to her bike.

But something kept her rooted to the warm barn. She watched Angie canter around the ring once, then head toward a vertical. They took off early, but cleared it nicely anyway. It was the oxer that followed, a parallel bar-type fence with two rails, which was going to give them trouble.

"Center him, Angie," she whispered, automatically tensing. "Center him."

Suddenly AB veered to the right and ran out, unleashing a string of curses from Angie. "You idiot!"

she cried. The crack of her riding crop against his flank
shattered the morning calm. "You think you're boss,
but you've got another think coming. I say jump, you
jump, AB."

She yanked on the reins, turning AB back with
such ferocity that Melissa winced. Again Angie took
the palomino through a preliminary canter around
the ring. Again they took the first vertical neatly,
although this time Angie was so busy using her crop
that she nearly lost her seat on their landing. She
turned AB toward the oxer, again, too tightly, ensuring
that the horse would have to take the fence at a sharp,
dangerous, and probably futile angle.

"Bad approach, Angie," Melissa whispered, clench-
ing her fists.

Flailing her crop against AB's shoulder, Angie drove
the frightened horse closer. Melissa could see the hot
fear in the horse's eyes as Angie bore him down, reins
clenched so tightly he could barely move his head, crop
crackling like wildfire.

Suddenly, so close he could nearly brush the fence
with his nose, AB angled sharply to the right, nearly
careening into the ring fence.

As they came to an abrupt halt, Angie was thrown
forward. She lunged for AB's neck and her legs flew
off in a tangle. She managed to hang on to his mane
for a split second before landing on the ground with a
dull thud.

As Melissa began running toward the ring, Angie

grabbed her crop and pulled herself up. Her face was twisted with rage. "Damn you!" she cried, "you stupid, ugly animal!"

Angie grabbed AB's reins to keep him in her reach. Her arm flew back and the crop came down on her terrified horse, again and again and again, slicing the air and landing, each time with a nauseating crack.

7

"Angie!" Melissa screamed. "Stop it! Stop it now!"

Angie spun around, the crop suspended in mid-air. AB took advantage of her momentary distraction to yank the reins free and gallop to the far side of the ring. He stopped there, snorting and dancing in fear, eyeing Angie warily.

Melissa threw open the gate. Without thinking, she grabbed the crop and wrenched it from Angie's grasp.

"What the—" Angie's gaze was laser hot. "Give me that now, or you'll regret it."

"How dare you treat a horse like that?" Melissa demanded, her voice choked with fury.

"He ran out twice. I was disciplining him. And I dare treat him that way because he happens to be mine."

"You weren't disciplining him, Angie, you were beating him. On the head, on the neck—" Melissa pointed to AB, watching the two of them like a cornered rabbit. "Look at him! He's scared to death!"

Hands on hips, Angie took a step forward. She was taller than Melissa by a foot, not to mention bigger, but Melissa stood her ground. "And where do you get off telling me what to do? Who are you, anyway," she said with a sneer at Melissa's filthy jeans and boots, "the manure patrol?"

Melissa gripped the crop with white-knuckled fury. She stared back at Angie for long seconds. What could make a seemingly normal person turn so cruel, so violent, in the space of an instant?

"It's my crop. It's my horse." Beneath the steel, there was a hint of fear in Angie's voice.

Melissa held out the crop. Angie snatched it away. "You can have the crop," Melissa replied. "But I promise you, if I have anything to say about it, you won't be able to keep the horse."

Melissa found Rose in her cluttered office, straightening one of the many antique horseshoes hanging on the walls. They shared space with plaques, ribbons, photos and memorabilia. Above her desk was a framed photo of Claire on Wishful Thinking, sailing over an uneven oxer at the Olympic equestrian trials.

Usually Melissa loved to linger over the clutter, the happy accumulation of a life lived with horses, but right now, all she could see as she barrelled into Rose's office was the horrifying image of Angie, whipping AB while he cringed in fear.

"Melissa!" Rose exclaimed. "You're still here, kiddo? You should be on your way to school by now." She glanced at the horse clock on her wall, the one with a wooden tail that swished back and forth like a pendulum. "Correction. You should be *at* school. You haven't been alphabetizing the tack room, have you?"

Melissa cleared a spot on the couch layered with horse magazines and unopened mail. She closed her eyes and gritted her teeth, waiting for the anger to pass. It didn't.

"Melissa, dear, what on earth has got you so riled?"

"Angie." She nearly spat out the name.

"Ah. Well, she's not particularly my favorite person, either."

"Rose, she just beat AB." Melissa fought back tears, remembering the horse's look of terror. "You've got to do something!"

"Whoa." Rose dropped into her desk chair across from Melissa. "Start from scratch."

"I was just out there by the training ring, about to leave. She was jumping the course—badly, by the way—and AB ran out a couple of times. The second time Angie more or less fell off, and all of a sudden she started belting him with her crop." Melissa steadied her voice. "I mean, his neck, his head, his shoulder! God, Rose, it was awful. I ran over and grabbed her crop out of her hand and she said . . . well, a few choice words . . . And then I came here." Melissa took a deep breath. "You have got to do something, Rose. Take AB away from her. Something."

Rose pursed her lips. She stood, glanced out the window, shook her head and began to pace—not an easy task, given the obstacle course of paperwork on her floor.

"Do you think AB was injured?" Rose asked.

"I don't know. He got free of her, so I didn't get a good look. I don't think so, though. At least, I hope not."

"In a way, it would almost be better if he were hurt."

"What?" Melissa demanded.

Rose sighed. "If AB were injured, I could go the ASPCA or even the police. There are laws against abusing animals. But as it is—as much as this pains me to say it—there's not a whole lot I can do, Melissa."

"But Rose, we can't just sit by and let her mistreat her horse this way—"

"If AB were one of Silver Creek's horses," Rose said grimly, "this would be a whole different matter. But he's not. He's a boarder's horse. That means that, within reason, Angie can treat her horse any way she wants to."

"This was *not* within reason," Melissa seethed. "This was brutal. I mean, Angie seemed okay when we first met her. And then, all of a sudden, it was like she snapped, Rose. You don't understand."

"Oh, but I do. I've seen it before, in owners who don't know how to communicate with their animals. They get frustrated, and instead of asking themselves what they're doing wrong, they blame the horse. The frustration builds up and that's how they find a release. It's inexcusable."

Melissa slumped back on the couch. She let out a long low breath, waiting for the knife edge of her own anger to blunt. "I keep seeing this look in AB's eyes," she whispered. "Like he was asking *What have I done?*" A tear burned her cheek. "I can't stand it, Rose. There has to be something we can do."

Rose put her hand on Melissa's shoulder. "First of all, I'm going to give Angie a warning. Not that anything I've had to say to her so far has done any good, not that she even has to listen. Second, I'm going to have a good look at that horse to see if there are any obvious signs he's been hurt. Beyond that, I guess the best we can do is keep an eye on Angie."

"It's AB we need to watch out for." Melissa picked at a piece of mud on her knee. "Couldn't you just, you know, kick her out? Kind of evict her?"

"Well, she has a six-month boarding contract, but yes, I could. We've got a waiting list for boarders two pages long." Rose took a sip of coffee from a mug on her desk. "But I'm not sure that's the best thing in this case."

"Why not? She should be punished," Melissa argued fervently.

"Because she'll just move on to another stable, hon. And maybe they'll be more tolerant of Angie's behavior. Maybe they won't have access to the best equine vet in the area. Maybe they won't care about AB the way you and I do."

Melissa stood. She threw back her shoulders and gazed out the window. "It isn't fair. Not to AB."

"I know it isn't. In an ideal world, only the most caring and deserving riders would have the privilege of owning a horse. But this, unfortunately, ain't an ideal world. Come on. Go grab that two-wheeled mount of yours and I'll drive you over to school."

"Thanks, Rose." Melissa checked her watch. "Unless we really crank, I'll miss math."

"Then by all means," Rose said with a conspiratorial wink, "we'd better stop and grab a donut on the way."

"But then I'll be sure to miss—"

"I see you're catching on."

While Rose warmed up her truck, Melissa went to the locker area and quickly changed into her school clothes. As she wheeled her bike past the stable, she caught a glimpse of Angie.

AB was cross-tied in the aisle and Angie was untacking him, muttering soundlessly while AB flinched at her every touch.

"Wow, she grooms her own horse, even," Jenna said Saturday as she cross-tied Big Red after their lesson. "I'd have thought Sharon was too big a local celebrity to bother with such grunt work."

"Would you be referring to Sharon, of the 'tumbling red mane like volcanic overflow'?" Katie asked.

"You want to see volcanic overflow, keep it up," Sharon warned.

"Despite that dry wit," Jenna said, "she really has a sweet inner charm."

"Enough already with that article," Sharon warned. For two days she'd endured phone calls and pats on the back from people who'd read the story about her miraculous soon-to-be comeback.

"It's nice, the way she still talks to us little people, isn't it?" Katie teased as she headed for the tack room.

Sharon reached for a dandy brush and began working down Blooper's dusty neck in even, gentle strokes. "Do you mind if I deliberately change the subject?"

"Yes," Jenna said. "I'm not done harassing you."

"My loss. It seems there's something strange going on here."

"Strange, how?" Melissa asked as she led Foxy, a piebald mare, down the aisle.

"Everything's too . . . I don't know. Organized." Sharon paused to scratch Blooper between the ears. "I mean, Rose has always been a stickler for neatness, but did you see how all the bridle hooks and saddle racks have been labeled with these little embossed cards in green Magic Marker?"

Katie returned, carrying a plastic tote full of grooming tools down to Say-So. "And how about those shelves next to the blankets and leg wraps?" she said. "Did you notice how everything's in alphabetical order? Saddle soap, sponges, sweat scrapers . . . it's eerie."

"They're not alphabetical," Jenna said. "Otherwise the shavers wouldn't have been on the top shelf."

"No, that's a *c*, for clippers," Katie argued. "Before currycombs and after braiding bands."

"Well, I think it's a wonderful system," Melissa said.

"You would," Sharon replied, gently working her way down Blooper's flank. "You alphabetize your sock drawer."

"They are not alphabetized, they are color-coded, light to dark. It makes dressing much faster in the morning."

"Well, anyway, I think Art needs to get a hobby," Jenna said. "Or, alternatively, a life."

"Actually, Rose said Art is cutting back on his hours," Katie said. "Something about going to college part-time."

"Did she say who took his place?" Melissa asked, looking over suddenly.

"Nope."

"Did you ask?" Melissa pressed.

Sharon paused to untangle a knot in Blooper's tail with her fingers. "Why, are you looking for a second career? Full-time A-plus student not enough?"

"Just curious." Melissa lingered in front of AB's stall. When she held out her hand and clucked softly, the palomino just eyed her nervously and tossed his head.

"He's a little skittish, isn't he?" Katie asked as she began carefully picking at Say-So's right front hoof. "I tried to say hello before our lesson and he practically freaked."

"Maybe he has reason to," Melissa said darkly.

"What do you mean?" Katie asked.

"Just that, well, I get the feeling Angie's not the gentlest rider in the world, to put it mildly."

Sharon dropped her dandy brush into her tote bucket. "When have you seen Angie riding?" she asked.

"I just, uh . . . it's just stuff I've heard. You know. Stuff."

"What kind of stuff?" Sharon asked.

"Stuff. Rumors." Melissa shrugged. "I don't know, Sharon, what is this, the Inquisition? Twenty Questions?"

"Jeez, Melissa, get a grip. I was just asking."

Melissa gave an uncomfortable grin. "Sorry. I don't know what my problem is. Terminal PMS, maybe."

"You're probably just wired about the show," Katie suggested.

"Yeah, probably," Melissa said softly. "Anyway. I've got to get going on Foxy. She's going to feel neglected. You three will be done grooming before I even get started." She started down the aisle. "Be right back. I'm going to get my grooming stuff."

"Just look under S," Jenna called.

"S?"

"For 'stuff.' "

Melissa rolled her eyes and headed for the tack room.

"By the way, don't even say the word *show* around me," Sharon said firmly. "I mean it. Let's have a moratorium on show talk."

"But I love talking about the show," Jenna protested. "It's all I can think about. I'm even using it as my excuse for the C-plus in history I got yesterday on the first pop quiz of the school year."

"I'm serious." Sharon leaned her head on Blooper's withers. He twisted his head as far as he could, giving her an annoyed snort. "All right, already, I'll keep brushing," she said with a grin. "Ever since that article came out, I have been deluged with calls. All these people wanting to say how inspired they were, and can they get tickets to watch my victorious return to the ring, blah, blah, blah."

"The price of fame," Jenna said, winking at Katie.

"No, really, I mean it. It's awful," Sharon said.

"What's awful?" Melissa asked as she returned from the tack room.

"That article," Sharon answered. "Guess who called me last night?"

"What is this, Twenty Questions?" Melissa teased.

"Okay, I'll tell you. Lucinda James."

"You're kidding." Melissa shook her head. "She came in third behind Sharon and me at the Classic that year. Really a tough competitor. And . . ."

"And?" Jenna prompted.

Melissa exchanged a look with Sharon. "And, well, she's kind of, well . . ."

"She's a card-carrying, toad-eating, hairy-warted witch," Sharon supplied.

"I was just going to say she's a little socially inept," Melissa said.

"Yeah, well, you're more discreet than I am."

"She has a beautiful Arabian gelding."

"I don't know why she needs him," Sharon said, "when she's got a perfectly serviceable broom." She fastened a loose tendril of hair back into her thick ponytail. "Anyway, Lucinda lives in New Hampshire, but someone around here called her and told her about the article, and then she decided she just had to call me and tell me she couldn't wait to see me at the show."

"The show!" Melissa exclaimed. "She's coming?"

"She has a great-aunt near here and Lucinda's going to be visiting for the weekend." Sharon let her voice fall into a singsong parody of Lucinda. "And she just can't *wait* to see me take the blue ribbon in my class . . . even if it *is* just a baby walk/trot. Why, Lucinda was six when she entered her first walk/trot class!" She groaned, recalling the condescending tone in Lucinda's high-pitched voice. "I should never, ever have done that stupid interview."

Claire entered the stable, a slip of paper in one hand. "I have the feeling this might not be the best time for me to bring this up," she said, stuffing the paper into her jeans jacket pocket.

"What?" Sharon asked.

"Never mind. It's about that article."

"Tell me."

"Don't bite my head off, Sharon," Claire warned, holding up a hand. "I just happened to answer the phone. I am an innocent phone-answering bystander."

She pulled out the piece of paper. "It seems that Randi Olander at PET read the article about you in the *Gazette*. Remember her? She's the program director."

"Sort of."

"Well, she called me to see if I'd ask you. I guess she figured, since you dropped out of the program, you probably wouldn't be all that receptive to her asking—"

"Asking what?"

"Randi was thinking it might be really inspirational to have you come down to the program sometime and give a little, you know, speech."

"A speech?" Sharon echoed incredulously.

"Not a speech, exactly, more like a talk. A chat. About how you've dealt with challenges, about what riding means to you, that sort of thing."

"Sharon, that's a great idea!" Katie exclaimed. "It would mean so much to those people to see how well you're doing."

"Nope. I don't give speeches. I don't even like to listen to speeches. As it happens, I'm allergic to speeches."

"That's what I told Randi," Claire said. "I said, no way will Sharon Finnerty get up in front of a group of people and give a speech. Not in this lifetime." She crumpled the paper into a ball. "I said, 'Randi, the day Sharon Finnerty does that, I'll ride naked through Miller Falls like Lady Godiva.'"

"Wait a minute." Sharon dropped her brush. "What do you mean, not in this lifetime?"

"Well, let's face it. You didn't even want to do that one-on-one interview. In what universe are you going to be giving speeches about yourself?" Claire leaned against a stall door, arms crossed over her chest. "Even if it could change somebody's life. Even if it could inspire someone to try just a little bit harder to get through another day of pain. I mean, you have your privacy to protect. You don't owe them the time of day."

Sharon gazed forlornly at her friends. "It's happening again, isn't it? I'm in some bizarre Twilight Zone time warp, aren't I? Once again I'm about to agree to something I really don't want to do because someone's trying pathetic child psychology on me."

Claire gave a small nod, a private acknowledgment that she'd known all along Sharon would come around. "I'll go call Randi."

"This is great, Sharon," Katie said. "You can practice on us tonight at the sleepover."

"We promise not to heckle you," Jenna vowed, grinning.

"Oh, Claire?" Sharon said as Claire turned to leave. "You know that stuff about Lady Godiva?"

"Hyperbole, that's called. Exaggeration for effect."

"Stupidity, that's called," Sharon replied with a sly smile. "Don't forget I have three witnesses."

8

"Can I give Charlotte some popcorn?" Sharon asked, peering at Katie's pet tarantula with a mixture of fascination and disgust. It was Saturday evening, and the Silver Creek Riders were gathered in Katie's kitchen, waiting for a second bag of microwave popcorn to finish popping.

"She only likes unbuttered," Katie said as she monitored the microwave. "Also, corn dogs. No mustard."

"I cannot believe this menagerie," Melissa commented, stroking the ears of Katie's big, sloppy dog, Beast. Beast drooled contentedly on Melissa's red terry cloth robe.

Jenna, who was perched on a counter, looked up from the book she was reading. "A cat, a dog, a tarantula, two aquariums full of fish, a lizard and four gerbils," she recited.

"Eight," Katie corrected. "Turned out George and Paul were really George and Paul*ette*."

"You forgot the partridge in a pear tree," Sharon said. She pulled at the edge of the blue facial mask drying on her face. "How much longer do I keep on this goop, anyway, Katie?"

"Don't peel!" Katie warned. "It hasn't sunk into your pores yet."

Sharon grimaced. "Are you sure that's a good idea? I'm not sure I want something sinking into my pores. What if it never comes *out* of my pores? What if I end up looking like this permanently?"

Melissa reached for her camera and snapped a shot of Sharon. "For the lawsuit," she explained. "Just in case."

"Melissa, you have a way of catching people in compromising positions," Jenna chided.

"She's still bitter over that picture you took the first day of camp," Katie said. "You know—right after she'd landed in a pile of goat turds."

"Hey, I don't make the events," Melissa said, shrugging. "I just document them."

"You think you could photograph me on Big Red at the show?" Jenna asked. "You know, in mid-air, like this?" She displayed the back cover of the book she was reading.

"What's that you're reading?" Melissa asked.

"It's called *Jump for Joy*. I thought I might pick up some fine points before the show." Jenna sighed. "Do you think I made a mistake, entering hunter jumping? Margaret and Claire say I'm ready, but still . . . Maybe I overdid it."

Sharon laughed. "I've been worrying that I under-did it, just entering walk/trot."

"None of those jumps will be over three feet, Jenna," Melissa said. "You'll be fine."

Katie pulled the second bag of popcorn from the microwave. "How about your class, Melissa? How tall are those?"

"None higher than three foot six," Melissa said, fingering the edge of her mask. She took the bag of popcorn from Katie and poured it into a big glass bowl. "Not that I have to worry," she added.

"What do you mean?" Katie asked.

"My mom laid the bombshell on me this afternoon after lessons," Melissa said lightly. "My aunt—you know the one who lives in New York City?—she's getting married. Guess when?"

Jenna slammed her book shut. "You don't mean you're missing the show!"

"There'll be other shows." Melissa gave a tight smile. It was hard to tell if it was because she was upset, or because her mask was beginning to harden. "You know how it is. Family stuff. I tried to argue, but there's no way I can get out of it. Besides, she's my favorite aunt."

"But this was going to be the first show we were all in together," Jenna cried. "All four of us. The Silver Creek Riders, united. Besides, I need you there for moral support, Melissa."

"Melissa's right, Jen," Sharon said, sending Melissa a sympathetic smile. "There'll be other shows."

"Still." Katie put her arm around Melissa's shoulders. "It's too bad. I know how excited you were about competing. And it won't be the same without you."

"Hey, I'll be there right up till you leave. I might

even be able to come by the morning of the show
and help you get ready so you don't totally lose it
to pre-show jitters," Melissa said. She laughed, but
Katie could see the beginning of tears in her dark
almond eyes.

"Anyway, like you say, it's just one show." Melissa
grabbed a handful of popcorn and headed for the hall.
"I don't care what you say, Katie," she said, "I have
got to wash this goop off before it gets permanently
attached. I'm going upstairs to the bathroom."

"You're supposed to peel, then wash," Katie cautioned, but Melissa was already hurrying away.

"Think she's okay?" Jenna whispered.

Sharon peeled some dried goop off her chin. "Ouch,"
she complained. "Is my chin still there?" She lowered
her voice. "I think she's fine. Melissa's been in a zillion
shows. I'm sure she's disappointed, but in a way, this
show is a bigger deal for you two—and I suppose for
me, come to think of it. Melissa's a pro."

"She looked upset, though," Katie said. "Do you
think I should go check on her?"

"Of course she's upset. She's got blue cement
plastered to her face," Sharon said, attempting to
peel her nose.

"It just won't be the same now," Jenna said
sullenly.

"I know," Katie said, "but we need to try to boost
Melissa's spirits. And Sharon's right. There'll be plenty
of other shows." She pulled four cans of soda from the
fridge. "We need to distract her with something fun."

"Ouija board? Truth or dare? Prank phone calls?" Jenna ticked the suggestions off on her fingers. "Or how about my personal favorite, porking out in front of the TV, watching a bad old movie? *Plan Nine from Outer Space* is on tonight at ten. It's like the worst movie ever made."

"I have another idea," Katie said. She hesitated. This could be potentially dangerous, involving her friends, but still . . .

"I got a letter today." Katie felt her usual blush begin to crawl up her neck. "From Matt."

"Matt Collier wrote you?" Jenna cried. "Let's see the goods. Is it a declaration of his undying love?"

"No, it's more like hi, how are you, I am fine. A declaration of his utter neutrality." Katie pulled a pad of paper out of a drawer. "So you'll help me write him back? Before I lose my nerve?"

"I don't know if this is such a good idea, Katie," Sharon said. "Last time Jenna tried to write letters, it wasn't exactly a literary triumph."

"That was different." Jenna grabbed a handful of popcorn, tossed a piece several feet into the air, and caught it in her mouth. "Melissa had just broken up with Marcus and I was inventing a secret admirer to get her out of her funk. This time, it's a real letter from a real, live person. Totally different situation."

"So do we get to read the actual letter?" Sharon asked.

Katie withdrew the envelope from her book bag in the corner of the kitchen. "Here," she said. "No sarcastic comments, please."

Sharon scanned it. "So?" Jenna prompted, tossing a piece of popcorn into Beast's mouth.

"So," Sharon said, "he's on the soccer team, he hates his English teacher, Romance has really improved her manners, and . . . oh yeah, he signed it *Love, Matt.* Not 'Like, Matt.' or 'Indifferently Yours, Matt.' Good sign."

Katie rummaged through her book bag. "I can't find a pen." She tried the junk drawer next to the fridge. "No luck."

"Here," Jenna said. "I'll bet Melissa has one in her purse. You know how organized she is. She probably has the entire Bic collection." She dug through Melissa's leather purse and pulled out a felt-tip marker.

"Green okay?" she asked. Then her eyes went wide. "Wait just a minute. Does this pen remind you of anything?"

Sharon and Katie exchanged a look. "The tack room," they both said at the same instant.

"The letter to Matt can wait," Katie said firmly. "We need to have a little talk with Melissa."

"Melissa!" Jenna's insistent voice filtered through the bathroom door. "You okay in there? You didn't drown, did you?"

Melissa stared at her reflection in the mirror. A little piece of mask clung to her right eyebrow. It was the face of a liar. A liar with nice, clean pores. *Tell the truth, you idiot*, Melissa instructed herself. *These are your friends.*

"Melissa?" Katie called. "Please come out. We need to talk."

She couldn't hide in the bathroom forever. Could she?

"Melissa? Did you peel yours yet?" Sharon knocked on the door loudly. "Because I peeled mine and I think some of my more vital pores may be missing. Also, a large segment of my left nostril."

Melissa laughed in spite of herself. She opened the door a tiny crack and the three of them poured in like a rushing tide.

"You lied," she said. "Your nostril's intact."

"Sharon's not the only one who lied," Jenna said, settling comfortably in the bathtub. "Exhibit A."

Melissa stared at the green felt-tip. "What were you doing in my purse?" she demanded.

"Looking for a pen so we could write Matt a heartfelt-but-not-too-committed letter," Sharon explained.

"You're the phantom alphabetizer in the tack room, aren't you?" Jenna asked.

"Melissa," Katie said gently as she sat cross-legged on the bath rug, "what's going on? You can tell us."

Melissa slumped down next to her. "I know. It's just so . . . I don't know. Embarrassing."

"How could you be embarrassed, talking to people with blue putty on their faces?" Jenna asked.

Melissa sighed. She thought of Rose's warning—

Three may keep a secret, if two of them are dead. One way or another, it was bound to come out eventually.

"I'm working mornings at the stable." The instant the words were out of her mouth, Melissa felt relieved. "My mom got laid off, and it's the only way I can keep taking lessons. I worked it out with Rose. Then I swore her to secrecy."

"But why?" Katie asked gently. "Why didn't you want to tell us?"

"I bet I know why." Jenna laid back and propped her feet up on the faucet. "I felt the same way at first when things fell through with Turbo. It's dumb, but you feel sort of embarrassed. Actually, it's *really* dumb, since I could care less how much money other people's parents have. I don't know why I thought other people would care about how much we had. So in the end, I just decided to stop worrying about it."

"Maybe that's part of it," Melissa said. "But I don't think it's the main thing. It's mostly that I just feel different, you know?" She gave an embarrassed smile. "Isolated. And I already sort of felt like the outsider."

"Why, Melissa?" Katie asked.

Melissa pushed back her sleeve and held her arm next to Katie's. "Well, to start with, near as I can tell, there's a slight shade variation between me and most of my friends."

"You think that's bad?" Sharon said. She sat up and put her face near Katie's. "Look at the girl. I'm white, she's blue." She pointed to the heavy plastic braces on her legs. "Plus I'm the only one who's made this interesting choice in legwear accessories."

Melissa smiled. "Well, it's not just that. I'm new here, from another state—"

"I moved here the middle of last year from Vermont," Sharon pointed out. "And I go to a different school, on top of that."

Melissa hesitated. "Then there's the fact that my parents are divorced," she said.

"So are mine," Katie pointed out. "And I'm the only one with a stepmother."

"Not to mention a tarantula," Jenna added.

Melissa played with the belt of her robe. "Wait a minute here. All of a sudden I'm starting to feel perfectly ordinary. I was afraid of everyone feeling sorry for me." She grinned. "And now I'm starting to feel sorry for all of you!"

Everyone laughed. "You know, we should have known it was you working at the stable," Jenna said. "The tack room's never looked better."

"I just started this week. There's a lot I still want to get done," Melissa said.

"It must be hard, getting up at that hour every day," Sharon said.

"Yeah, but the truth is, I kind of like it. The stable's magic that time of day. All the horses are so glad to see you, and it's so peaceful. You notice things you wouldn't see the rest of the time."

Suddenly she recalled the horrible scene with Angie and AB. "Sometimes you see things you wish you hadn't seen," she added darkly. "Yesterday morning, just as I was about to leave, I saw Angie beating AB with her crop after he ran out on a jump." She shuddered at the memory. "It was awful. Brutal. I tried to stop her, then I went to Rose."

"What did she say?" Katie asked.

"Basically, that there was nothing we could do unless he was seriously hurt, since Angie's just a boarder." Melissa sighed. "Rose felt as bad about it as I did, believe me. Today before our lesson she told me she had a serious talk with Angie, who pretty much just blew Rose off. Rose checked over AB and he seemed fine, and she even called Angie's parents."

"What did they say?" Jenna asked.

"That their sweet little angel of a daughter could never do such a thing, and Rose should mind her own business."

"There must be something else we can do," Katie moaned. "That beautiful palomino. I can't stand to think of him being treated that way."

"I'd like to think that it won't happen again, now that Rose and I have talked to Angie," Melissa said. "But something about her attitude . . . I don't know. I just have the feeling it won't be the last time."

"What kind of parent allows a kid to treat an animal that way?" Jenna demanded. "It makes me sick. Too bad you don't have some kind of proof—"

"Wait a minute," Melissa said, snapping her fingers. "What if we *did* have proof?"

"What kind of proof?" Katie asked. "Even if we had

a dozen witnesses, Angie's parents are going to believe whatever she tells them."

"You know what they say," Melissa said slyly. "A picture's worth a thousand words."

"Your camera!" Sharon exclaimed.

"At last," Jenna added, "you can use your photographic power for good instead of evil."

"We'll all keep an eye on her," Melissa said. She smiled with relief. "I feel so much better. At least this way I can do something. Plus, I don't have to keep that secret any longer. I have to admit, it was starting to eat away at me."

"Speaking of eating away," Katie said nervously, peering into the mirror. She yanked at a corner of her mask with no effect. "You don't think you can leave these things on *too* long, do you?"

"Oh, this is not *too* obvious," Melissa muttered the following Saturday as she and her three friends trotted, four abreast, across a wide green field. In the distance, Angie, riding AB, was nearing a fork in the trail.

"Do you think she's noticed us yet?" Katie asked.

"She's got four thousand-pound animals hot on her trail, Katie," Sharon said. "I'd say odds are she's probably caught on by now."

At the fork, Angie stopped. She turned around in her saddle, staring back across the field.

"We'd better cool it," Melissa said, reining in Big Red.

"If she asks, what will we say?" Katie said.

"That we just wanted to go out for a little trail ride after our lesson was finished," Jenna replied reasonably. "Exactly what we told Claire."

"Yeah, and she didn't buy it, either," Sharon pointed out.

Melissa checked her camera, which she had strapped around her waist inside her down vest so it wouldn't bother her while she rode. "Come on, Angie," she whispered. "You're on Candid Camera."

"I think she knows," Katie said. "That's why she's on her best behavior."

"That's good, though," Melissa said. "At least that means AB's okay."

Suddenly Angie legged AB into a gallop. A moment later, she disappeared behind a ridge of trees.

"After her!" Melissa shouted.

They flew across the field at a joyous, all-out gallop. The incredible burst of speed, the wind biting at her cheeks, the first touch of scarlet in the maples . . . Melissa was enjoying the ride so much that she almost forgot that this ride wasn't about fun. She was on a mission. A mission that, despite her best efforts, had been thwarted all week.

She wanted to believe that Angie had been scared off by Rose's blunt warning, and perhaps even by the confrontation with Melissa—wanted to believe it for AB's sake. But yesterday morning, Melissa had been coming out of the feed room when she'd heard Angie screaming, her voice echoing in the indoor ring.

Melissa had dashed to the ring to find Angie

standing nose-to-nose with AB, shaking her fist at him. When she'd registered Melissa's presence, Angie had conjured up a smile as slow as a glacier and just as cold. "You need something?" she'd asked.

"Is everything okay in here?" Melissa had demanded.

"Not that it's any of your business, but yes," Angie had replied. "We were just having a little heart to heart, AB and I."

It wasn't exactly enough to convict her, Melissa knew. Yelling at an animal who didn't understand what you wanted might be irrational and counterproductive, not to mention cruel. But you couldn't take a photo of cruel words.

When they reached the base of the ridge, Melissa signaled them to halt. "This is crazy," she said. "Angie's too smart to let herself get caught out here. Let's take it easy the rest of the way."

By the time they'd cooled down and reached the stable, Angie was already grooming AB at the far end of the aisle. She gave them a haughty half-smile as she yanked a comb through AB's tail.

"There," Jenna whispered as she cross-tied Turbo. "Did you see the way she was grooming him? Way too rough."

Melissa undid her jacket and discreetly readied her camera. "Well, it's not much," she said. "But I might as well use up the film."

She stepped into Turbo's stall and trained the camera on Angie, peering over the top of the door while she tried her best to look inconspicuous. Fortunately, Angie seemed to be too busy rushing through AB's grooming to notice Melissa.

Melissa, her eye glued to the viewfinder, felt someone next to her before she realized who it was. "I don't suppose you'd like to let me in on what you're up to with that camera?" Claire inquired.

Melissa nearly dropped it. "Claire! I was just, um, don't you think this would make a nice shot, the sun coming through the stable door, AB over there getting spruced up—"

"Not to mention Angie doing the sprucing," Claire finished. She crossed her arms. "She told me you four followed her, Melissa," Claire said in a low voice. "Now, no one's more sympathetic to what you're trying to do than I am. But you can't harass the boarders. You've got to be a little more discreet. Get it?"

Melissa nodded. "Got it."

"And even if you did get something on film, I'm not sure how that's going to help," Claire continued.

"We thought it might convince Angie's parents she doesn't deserve to own a horse," Jenna whispered.

Claire frowned. "Well, just don't take it too far, okay?"

"Who knows?" Melissa said with a thoughtful sigh. "Maybe Angie's reformed. Rose did give her a big lecture."

"Hey, speaking of big lectures," Claire said, looking over at Sharon, "did you set up a date for your PET talk?"

"Next week," Sharon said. "Don't ask me what I'm going to say."

"What are you going to say?" Claire asked, grinning.

Sharon just rolled her eyes.

"Promise me you four will keep your detective work under control?" Claire asked, turning back to Melissa.

"I promise." Melissa put the lens cap on her camera. "Besides," she added with a resigned smile, "the light in here's lousy."

9

The Program for Equestrian Therapy was located in an unassuming little stable near the outskirts of Miller Falls. As Sharon climbed out of her mom's car on a vibrantly clear Wednesday afternoon, a wave of uneasy recognition washed over her. This was the site of her first, halting efforts at learning to ride again. This little white stable, with its cadre of physical therapists and dedicated volunteers, with its ten gentle, sweet-tempered horses, was not a place she'd planned on ever returning to.

At least, she reminded herself, she'd had the good sense to bring her friends along.

"I'm so glad you guys are here," Sharon said, throwing back her shoulders and taking a deep breath of the piney air. She waved as her mother pulled out of the long drive.

"Hey, it was this or do English homework," Jenna said cheerfully. "Diagramming sentences, no less."

"I never even knew this place was here," Katie said as they started toward the low-slung stable.

"They pretty much survive on donations," Sharon explained. "And volunteers help out a lot."

"How many kids will be there today?" Melissa asked.

"Eight or nine, Randi said. From age three to sixteen." Sharon paused by the white gate surrounding the property. "I guess I should explain a little, to prepare you. This isn't like a normal riding class. These kids all have physical disabilities. Cerebral palsy, multiple sclerosis, spina bifida, paralysis. Or maybe an accidental injury, like mine. Sometimes they have emotional disabilities, too. Autism, maybe, or they might be learning disabled." She bent down to adjust her left brace. Her legs had a way of twinging whenever she was under stress.

"So these are like very basic riding lessons, then?" Jenna asked.

"Well, not exactly." Sharon stood, gripping the fence for support. Was it too late to back out now? She felt like she was being sucked into the past, a churning whirlpool of anger and unhappiness that she'd struggled long and hard to escape.

"Sharon!" Randi Olander emerged from the stable. Her black hair, tied back in a French braid, was longer, but she approached them with the same purposeful enthusiasm and ear-to-ear smile Sharon remembered.

"So good to see you!" Randi gave her a brief hug. "Claire tells me you're doing wonderfully."

"Randi Olander, meet Jenna, Katie and Melissa. They came along for moral support. They all ride with me over at Silver Creek."

"Excellent!" Randi rubbed her palms together. "It just so happens we're short on volunteers today. Flu's starting early this year, I guess. I don't suppose I could coerce you into helping out?"

"Sure," Melissa said. "What do we do?"

"Well, it's very simple, really. The whole theory behind hippotherapy is that we're using the horse's repetitive gait to provide sensory input. The horse moves you in three dimensions, as I'm sure you've noticed—up-down, side-to-side, forward-backward. Well, for these kids, that movement can help reeducate muscles. It's also very relaxing—the warmth of the horse, the repetition."

"So what do we do?" Katie asked.

"Well, we're pretty much tacked up already," Randi said. "You'll notice we do use some special equipment—hand-holds, neckstraps, sometimes a waist belt or a fleece pad. And a few of our clients use Devonshire boots—that's a special type of stirrup that helps stabilize the foot and keep it from sliding all the way through. It helps a lot with our kids with cerebral palsy who have tight heel cords." Randi motioned them toward the stable entrance. "What the volunteers do is either lead the horse around the ring or walk along either side at the rider's knee, reassuring the rider or helping with special exercises the therapist suggests."

"Sounds easy enough," Jenna said.

"It is. It's fun for the volunteers. And the kids just live for this. We've seen amazing changes in so many of them."

Randi led them to the ring behind the stable. Next to the ring was a small set of bleachers filled with observers.

"Parents, mostly," she explained. "It helps reassure the kids to have them here. Some of our riders are very anxious at first, until they get used to the feeling of height and the movement."

"That I remember very well," Katie said, grinning.

"You'll love our horses. They're just like big teddy bears, they're so sweet." Randi smiled knowingly. "I think that must have been a real frustration for you, right, Sharon?"

Sharon nodded. "I guess."

"Sharon was too advanced a rider to be participating here for long," Randi continued, almost as if Sharon weren't there. "That's why we're so thrilled to have her back to talk to these kids. Certainly most of them won't ever be the rider she is, but I'm sure she'll be an inspiration."

"Um, Randi?" Sharon tugged at her jacket. "Could I talk to you for a sec?"

"Sure." Randi pointed toward the stable. "Our volunteers could probably use some help leading out the horses, if you girls don't mind. We use a mounting ramp in the ring for our riders. Just ask for Martha."

Katie gave Sharon a thumbs-up sign. "We'll see you in a minute, Sharon."

"This is so nice of you, Sharon," Randi said as the others headed off. "What do you think you'll talk about? I thought maybe a little riding demonstration

would be a great idea. Just a few circles around the
ring."

Sharon watched as a mother wheeled a little boy in
a wheelchair up the drive. "I'm not exactly sure this is
a good idea, Randi."

"Why not?"

"To begin with, I don't have any idea what to say
to those kids."

"Tell them the truth. What it was like to get hurt,
how riding helped you get better. Tell them why you
love horses." Randi shrugged. "I'm not sure it matters
so much *what* you tell them. It's enough just to see
you."

"But seeing me ride . . . Won't that just make them
feel worse? I mean, most of them will never reach my
level of skill, you said so yourself."

My level of skill, Sharon repeated silently. As if
that meant anything, in the *real* world of riding.

Randi shook her head firmly. "You're one of them,
Sharon. You give them hope. You give them something
to shoot for."

"But I'm not," Sharon said, almost pleading. "I'm
not one of them, not anymore."

"Sharon." Randi's smile had lost some of its luster.
"Trust me. Just say hello and trot around the ring.
That will be plenty."

"Hi, everybody." Sharon cleared her throat. In the
front row of bleachers, nine young faces were trained
on her expectantly. She registered a blur of crutches,

two wheelchairs, a special helmet, assorted braces. That was enough. She didn't want to meet their eyes.

Behind her, Jenna, Katie and Melissa stood near the entrance to the ring, holding the horses that would be used for today's class. Sharon had selected one, an aging Appaloosa gelding, to use as her mount.

"And this—" she led the Appaloosa over to the fence near the bleachers, "as I guess most of you know, is Spot." She stroked him between the ears and he let out a contented sigh. "Spot and I go way back," Sharon continued. Her voice was a thin fly-buzz in her own ears. Could they hear her? Was she even making sense?

"See, I used to be a rider here. Spot was the first horse I rode after my . . . after I got hurt. And I was kind of nervous, you know, even though I used to ride horses a lot. I looked at Spot and I thought, geez, he's so big and my legs—" she pointed to her braces, "are so small, and if I fall, well, it's a long way down. I mean, he *seemed* like a nice enough guy, but how did I know he wasn't going to do something stupid—like step on me?"

Spot chose that moment to let out a derisive snort. Everyone laughed and Sharon realized with a start that yes, these people *were* actually listening to her.

"Well, it turned out Spot was just the right horse for me. He was kind and tolerant and even though my legs weren't very cooperative, I found out I could ride him and feel safe. With some help, of course. Spot here helped me remember why I loved riding."

For the first time, Sharon met the eyes of her front-row audience. "See, when you're riding, you get to move in a way you can't when you're just being a plain old person. Even if you're a person like . . . a person who can't move as easily as other people. It doesn't matter. You could be the fastest sprinter in the world or the highest jumper, and a just plain average horse can still do so much more. When you're on a horse, he lets you be like he is for a little while. Stronger and bigger and faster and more graceful."

She rubbed her cheek against Spot's smooth, warm neck and breathed in his sweet scent. "And you know what?" Sharon said softly. She wasn't even thinking about her listeners anymore. "I think the horse doesn't mind sharing a little bit of his magic with us. He gets something back from us, too."

A little girl wearing a thick blue helmet raised her hand. "What does the horse get?"

Sharon looked over, surprised. "Well, he gets our love. And our respect. He gets us to take care of him and hug him and groom him and take him to the vet and do all those things he can't do himself. That's a pretty fair deal, don't you think?" The little girl nodded. "But mostly," Sharon said, "I kind of like to think he enjoys showing off for us, you know?" She paused. "I had . . ."

Sharon fought the catch in her throat. She looked behind her, saw her friends, and pushed the words out. "I had a horse, a really beautiful horse." Spot nudged her shoulder. "Nothing personal, Spot. You're not bad yourself. But Cassidy was . . . well, she was really special. She loved to show off, like she wanted to be sure I knew how amazing she was. We were in an accident, Cass and I. That's how my legs got hurt. And . . ." Sharon let a tear fall, not caring who saw it. "And she died. When that happened I thought I would never ride again, never. But then I came here to PET, and there was Spot, looking at me with those big brown eyes." Sharon brushed her cheek with her sleeve. "And then he talked to me—"

"*Please*. Horses don't talk," a fragile-looking boy in a wheelchair interjected.

"Spot does," Sharon replied. "You just have to listen. He's a little shy." Several kids giggled, and for the first time, Sharon felt herself smile back. "Spot said to me, he said, *Sharon, I'm no Cassidy. I've got a bit of a pot belly and my jumping days are definitely over, but climb on board and you'll feel like you're flying, I promise.* So I did. And we walked around the ring in a circle. And for the first time in months I didn't have to think about my messed-up legs because Spot was doing all the work. And you know what? I think it may have been just about the best ride I ever took."

She hesitated. Spot looked at her expectantly. She hadn't even thought about this old bag of bones, not until today. Spot had just been a symbol of what she couldn't do, and as soon as she could leave his sagging old horse self behind, she had.

So why was she telling these kids these things, things she didn't really believe?

"I guess I'm done," Sharon said with a shrug. Suddenly she felt embarrassed—for her emotions, for her lousy speech. She looked at Randi. Sharon had warned her she'd let them down, and of course she had.

But just then Randi leapt to her feet, applauding furiously, and soon the rest of the audience was joining in. "How about a little demonstration now, Sharon?" Randi suggested, and the kids yelled their approval.

Someone passed her a hard hat, and, with a half-hearted smile, Sharon put it on. She felt her usual self-consciousness about mounting, then realized it didn't matter. These were kids who could barely sit in a saddle. What did they care about technique?

She made it up into the saddle on her second try. "Sometimes getting on the horse is hard for me," she admitted, "because my legs aren't very strong, you know?"

She looked down at the front row, at the legs and arms and spines that would not, most of them, ever get much better. They knew, all right. They knew much better than she did.

Sharon took Spot around the ring, first at a walk, then at a sitting trot. When she posted a figure eight, the audience gasped and applauded as if she'd just finished a flawless jump course at the Olympics. She felt a little foolish. Her friends, of course, knew better. They could see all the flaws, the poor heel position, the rigid posture.

After a few more turns around the ring, she brought

Spot to a halt and dismounted. The kids cheered and applauded, and some of them—those who could—even stood.

Sharon walked out of the ring quickly, feeling like a ridiculous fraud. "You were super," Randi said. "Just super." She gestured toward the bleachers. "Why don't you take a rest? We've got enough side-walkers, and you're probably tired."

"Yeah, I am, actually," Sharon said, taking off her hard hat.

"I don't suppose I could talk you into coming back on a regular basis?" Randi said.

"I don't think so," Sharon said quickly. "It's just not . . . I don't belong here. Not anymore."

For the next hour, Sharon sat on the bleachers, watching as her friends worked with the other volunteers and therapists. Mostly, they walked the horses around the ring in slow, steady circles. Sometimes they would bring them to a halt and the children would attempt basic exercises, reaching for a large plastic ring, perhaps, or bending forward at the waist to give the horse's neck a "hug."

After a while, Sharon stopped watching. It was too easy to imagine the pain and frustration that went with each stretch and bend. Too easy to look at those kids and imagine all the things they'd never be able to do.

She was roused from her thoughts by a boy's soft voice. "It's not the same," he said, almost fiercely.

At the other end of the bleachers, a boy, maybe ten or so, was watching the proceedings sullenly. He wore short braces like Sharon's, and a set of crutches lay nearby.

"Excuse me?" Sharon said.

"It's not the same." The boy glared at her. He had a sandy crew cut and a seen-it-all look in his dark eyes. "What you said about the riding. It's not the same as flying or anything else. Look at them."

Sharon looked. He was right, actually. A carousel horse would be more challenging.

"Is that why you're not riding?" Sharon asked.

The boy turned his stare back to the ring. "Yeah. My p. t. wants me to come, so my mom makes me. But I just sit." He gave a flinty smile. "It really burns them."

Sharon recognized the smile. "I used to fight my physical therapist too. It was pretty stupid, now that I think about it. But very satisfying."

The boy looked at her. "Exactly."

"So I take it you used to ride, huh?" Sharon said.

The boy gave a little half-shrug, half-flinch. "Nah. I had a black BMX bike. Better than a horse."

"Nothing's better than a horse."

"You ever had a BMX?"

"No," Sharon admitted.

"Then you shouldn't mouth off."

"Still," Sharon persisted, not sure why she was bothering, "you ought to try it sometime."

"No way." The boy fingered his aluminum crutch, a dull silver sheen in the waning afternoon light. "They're losers. I'm not like them."

Sharon watched Katie hug the leg of a little girl on a chestnut mare who'd just completed a successful turn around the ring. "Yeah," she said at last. "I guess I know what you mean."

10

On Friday morning, Melissa surveyed the feed room with satisfaction. She'd marked the tops of each of the hard plastic garbage cans with embossed labels. *Sweet feed, corn, crimped oats, barley* . . . It would make things go that much more efficiently at feeding time. She checked her watch. Right on schedule, with a few minutes to spare. But not enough time, unfortunately, to do much spying.

Angie was here again this morning, forcing AB through his paces in the outdoor training ring. So far, after many days of trying, Melissa and her friends had managed to annoy Angie to the point where she'd complained about their behavior twice to Rose and once to Claire. Rose had even gone so far as to give Melissa the three-strikes-and-you're-out-of-a-job warning.

Still, despite the lack of evidence—and the threat to the job she loved—Melissa was determined to keep a close eye on Angie. She was convinced that someone capable of such cruelty wouldn't suddenly reform overnight. Of course, she was also aware that Angie had plenty of time alone with AB out

127

on the trails when no one from Silver Creek could monitor her. It was even possible that the reason Angie was treating AB more decently was precisely because Jenna, Katie and Melissa were hounding her like rookie detectives.

As Melissa headed to the locker area, she noticed a woman in a shiny black Mercedes pull up. She emerged, sporting a thick fur coat, and headed over to the ring where Angie was cooling down AB. Angie's mom, Melissa decided. She had the same sleek blond haircut and take-charge walk.

When she was done changing into her school clothes, Melissa slipped her camera into her backpack. These days, she carried her camera to the stable every morning, just in case she caught Angie in some compromising moment.

Yesterday after school she'd picked up the first developed roll. She couldn't wait to show Katie and Jenna the results of their intensive surveillance. As she thumbed through the pictures, Melissa had to admit it was a pretty ridiculous collection, all things considered. Angie, scowling as she picked AB's hooves . . . Angie, hands on hips, screaming at AB in the indoor ring . . . Angie, giving the girls an obscene gesture as she galloped down a trail.

Not exactly enough evidence for conviction. Still, Melissa's gut told her not to give up quite yet.

She put the envelope of photos into the pocket of her down vest and slipped her backpack over her shoulder. Pausing in the stable doorway, she let her gaze roam over the horses munching contentedly. In the shafts of pale, dusty morning light, their coats shimmered. This was her favorite part of the job, this serene moment each morning before she left for school, when she paused to remind herself what all her hard work was buying.

Melissa grabbed her bike and made a wide arc around the training ring. She was almost to the drive when she heard a woman's commanding voice cut the air. "Young lady! I'd like a moment of your time."

Melissa braked. For a brief instant she considered the possibility that Angie's mother wanted to hear the real scoop on her daughter. But that seemed pretty unlikely, not to mention naïve.

She turned her bike around and walked it back. "Yes?" Melissa said, meeting Mrs. Marquette's cold gaze.

"My daughter tells me you've been harassing her."

"Did she also tell you she beats her horse?" Melissa demanded.

"Angie would never treat an animal that way," Mrs. Marquette said as Angie led AB over to the rail.

Melissa shook her head. "I saw it with my own eyes."

"Then perhaps," Mrs. Marquette said, "you should consider corrective lenses." She narrowed her eyes. "What exactly is it you *do* here?"

"She picks up manure," Angie volunteered.

"I also ride here," Melissa countered.

"Well, you won't be riding here *or* working here for much longer, if you don't leave my daughter alone."

"I'm telling you, she's not treating that horse right," Melissa said. "And as long as that's the case, I'll keep hounding her until I can prove it."

As she hopped onto her bike to leave, Melissa's backpack slipped off one arm. She reached back to adjust the strap, and something fell from her pocket.

Melissa stared at the ground, aghast. The photos of Angie lay there like a deck of cards tossed to the wind.

"What on earth?" Mrs. Marquette demanded. "Why, these are of Angie! All of them!"

"I told you she had a camera," Angie cried. "I saw it last week, in the stable."

Her mother bent down delicately, lifting up a photo between two fingers as if it were contaminated. "What would possess you to do such a thing?"

"I . . ." Melissa considered spinning an elaborate lie, something about a school project, perhaps. But she'd done more than her share of lying lately.

"I was trying to catch Angie on film," she said defiantly. "To prove what she's been doing, so you'd believe me."

"What I believe is that you are a seriously disturbed young lady," Mrs. Marquette said.

The door to the stable office opened and Rose appeared, coffee mug in hand. "I take it there's a problem?" she said grimly.

"These—" Angie's mother spread her arms to encompass the scattered photos, "*these* are the problem."

Rose picked up a photo of Angie combing AB's tail. "Well, yes, the composition's a little shoddy, but—"

"I fail to see the humor in this, Mrs. Donovan," Mrs. Marquette seethed.

"*I* fail to see why the composition's bad," Melissa added.

"This . . . employee . . . of yours has been systematically stalking my poor child! I've complained repeatedly, and I was assured you would control her behavior."

Rose stared into her mug, sighing deeply. "As it happens, I did speak to Melissa."

"Well, as it happens, she obviously didn't listen."

Rose looked at Melissa regretfully. "No, unfortunately, she didn't."

Melissa swallowed. The pained look in Rose's face said it all. "Three strikes," she said softly. "I know, Rose. It's okay."

"You should have fired her a long time ago," Angie said.

"I'm just going to say one more thing," Rose said evenly. "Melissa took things too far, yes. But she's a fine girl and a fine rider. I believe she told the truth about what she saw. And if you ever hurt that horse on my premises, boarder or not, you'll be out of here so fast you won't know what hit you. Got it?"

Without waiting for an answer, Rose put her arm

around Melissa and walked her away. "It's my own fault, Rose," Melissa admitted. "I know I went too far."

"Hon, you didn't leave me any choice. I'm truly sorry. How about if we work out something else? We could give you credit on some lessons, just until your mom's back on her feet financially. Goodness knows with all the extra work you've done around here, I probably owe you a year's worth."

Melissa gritted her teeth. She was not going to cry. At least not now. "No," she said firmly. "No charity. Besides, I'll be back here before you know it. You can't get rid of me this easily."

"You're a great kid, Melissa. I know you were just trying to do the right thing. Maybe down the road, when things calm down around here, you can—"

"It'll work out, Rose." Melissa forced a smile and pushed her bike toward the drive. A chill gust of wind sent something brushing up against her leg.

Melissa looked down to see a photo of Angie. She was galloping down a sun-touched trail, her hand outstretched in an obscene gesture, a fierce, defiant smile on her face.

"It's not fair," Jenna said, for what may have been the hundredth time since they'd heard the news about Melissa the previous day. She reined in Big Red near the spot where Sharon and Katie were watching. Their regular lesson over, Sharon had volunteered to give Jenna a few pointers on jumping in the indoor ring.

"This bites in a major way," Jenna added for emphasis.

"I just don't see how Rose could have done this," Katie agreed.

"She's a businesswoman, Katie," Sharon said. "She has a business to run. And you have to admit, she did give us all plenty of warning."

"But Melissa was just trying to do what's right," Katie insisted.

She'd spent last evening on the phone with Melissa, trying to convince her to attend today's lesson. Between the three of them, Katie had assured her, they could somehow manage to put together enough money to cover the cost of lessons for a while.

But Melissa had been just as adamant: no charity, under any circumstances. She'd find another job, after school, maybe. And her mother would be sure to find a new job soon. But until then, she would just have to give up on riding. It was not, she'd insisted, the end of the world. But Katie knew better. For Melissa, it might as well have been.

"What really burns me," Jenna said under her breath as she ran her fingers through Big Red's silky mane, "is that it's Angie who shouldn't be riding."

Sharon sighed. "You want to take a couple runs around the course, Jen? Then let's call it quits. I have to admit, I'm not exactly in the mood to think about the show. Especially now, after everything that's happened."

"One more time," Jenna said.

Claire had set up a model jump course of six fences that would roughly duplicate the course for Jenna's Hunters Over Fences class. None was over three feet, and the turns were wide and maneuverable. But the course looked plenty intimidating to Katie, who'd so far only tackled cavalletti, low ground rails set out between two wooden X's.

"Remember, Jenna, this is *not* a jumper class, where the fastest clear round wins," Sharon said. "This is a hunter class. The judges will be looking for a nice, steady pace and smooth form."

"I know, I know," Jenna said, rolling her eyes.

"Well, sometimes you get so aggressive with Red, you'd think you were in the jump-off at the National," Sharon teased. "Think style, not speed."

While Jenna took Big Red through the course smoothly, Margaret entered the ring and joined them.

"Looking good, Jenna," she called as Red carved a perfect arc over a post and rail. "Think ahead now. Anticipate that next jump so Red will, too. He's going to sense where you're looking. Atta girl."

"How'd the talk at PET go the other day, Sharon?" Margaret asked.

"I'm just glad it's over," Sharon said dismissively.

"She was great," Katie said. "Those kids were so enthralled when she spoke."

"Katie means no one fell asleep or threw rotten tomatoes at me," Sharon explained.

"They do great work over there," Margaret said.

"It was so much fun, Jenna and I are thinking of volunteering regularly," Katie said.

Jenna sailed neatly over the final jump. Her face was flushed with exertion, her bangs glued to her damp forehead.

"You're going to whiz through the show course with flying colors," Margaret assured her as she trotted over.

"That's what Melissa told me, too." Jenna brushed her brow with the back of her arm. "You're both optimists, though. She also thinks things will work out for the best with Angie and AB."

"How's Melissa holding up?" Margaret asked.

"She says she's fine," Katie replied.

"Even though the powers-that-be at Silver Creek betrayed her," Jenna added darkly.

Margaret gave a grim smile. "Nobody feels worse about this than Rose, Jenna."

"Then she should kick Angie out and give Melissa her job back," Jenna said firmly.

"Believe me, we powers-that-be have talked about that. A lot. The problem is, we need evidence," Margaret said. She tapped her chin thoughtfully. "Proof."

"That's what Melissa was trying to get," Katie argued.

"There's got to be a better way to go about it, though," Margaret said.

The side door to the arena opened, revealing Gary, ringed by bright sunlight. "I'm heading back to the clinic," he called to Margaret. "Should be home about six."

"Wait a sec, Gar." Margaret winked at the girls. "I believe we just met our 'better way,' ladies," she whispered.

Gary sauntered over, vet bag in hand. "Why do I have the feeling I'm stepping into the middle of a conspiracy?"

"I just hatched a brilliant idea," Margaret said, linking arms with her husband.

Gary sighed. "That would be my cue to run for cover."

"It's for a good cause, Gar."

"I think I get it," Katie said, smiling at Margaret.

"Why don't you explain it to my dear, sweet, remarkably cooperative husband, Katie?"

"Could someone fill me in, please?" Jenna said.

"Me too," Gary agreed.

"Why couldn't *you* take a look at AB, Gary?" Katie asked excitedly. "If you found even the tiniest symptom of abuse, it might be enough to convince Angie's parents there's a real problem—"

"Katie, that's brilliant!" Sharon exclaimed.

"Wait a sec," Margaret protested. "Don't *I* get any credit here?"

"Whoa." Gary made a time-out sign. "Before you go trying to grab credit, I need some more information here. Are we talking about that palomino Melissa saw being abused a while back?"

Margaret nodded.

"Sorry, folks." Gary shook his head regretfully. "The problem is, AB is not one of my clients. And since Angie's just boarding him at Silver Creek, the only way I could examine AB would be if there were some pressing medical emergency. This just doesn't qualify."

"Aha! But your wily wife has a solution to that," Margaret said.

"Yes, wily wife?" Gary crossed his arms over his chest.

"Well, you *are* the official vet for the Autumn Horse Show," Margaret pointed out. "A show Arkansas Breeze just happens to be entered in. Therefore, you have a vested interest in his condition, don't you?"

Gary nodded slowly, considering. "Not bad, not bad."

"Not bad?" Katie cried. "It's brilliant!"

"Now, don't get carried away," Gary cautioned. "I would have to find some kind of conclusive evidence of abuse, and apparently, as far as everyone can see, AB's a perfectly healthy horse." He shrugged. "Still, it's worth a try. Just realize that there's a good chance all I'll manage to do is annoy Angie."

"Like I said." Katie nodded. "Brilliant."

11

"Melissa! What took you so long?" Jenna cried, exploding from the stable as Melissa rode up on her bike.

"Are you kidding? I think I broke the speed limit back on Milford Drive!" Melissa replied, panting. She leaned her bike against the stable wall. "Will you please tell me what's going on?"

"It's about AB and Angie," Jenna said, gesturing toward the stable. "Follow me."

Inside, Melissa was surprised to find Margaret, Sharon and Katie gathered around AB's stall. Gary Stone was in the stall with AB, his vet bag open, his stethoscope draped around his neck.

"It was Margaret's idea—Margaret and Katie's," Jenna explained as Melissa hurried down the aisle. "Since Gary's the official vet for the Autumn Horse Show, he can legitimately examine AB to see if he's fit to be ridden. We thought if he found anything suspicious . . ." She shrugged. "Who knows? It's worth a shot."

"It's good to see you here today, Melissa," Margaret said, patting her on the back.

Melissa nodded. She felt odd being here at the stable, like an uninvited guest at a private party.

"We missed you at lessons," Katie added.

"It wasn't so bad," Melissa said. "For the first time in ages, I got to sleep in on a Saturday morning and watch moronic cartoons with Thomas."

"So far, so good, Melissa," Gary pronounced. "From what I can see, AB looks fine."

"Well, that's good news," Melissa said, sighing with relief. As much as she wanted to separate Angie from this beautiful horse, she didn't even want to think about the possibility that he might have suffered some kind of permanent damage at Angie's hands.

They watched as Gary positioned himself on AB's near side, next to the horse's shoulder. He stood very still, then quickly jerked a finger toward AB's eye.

"Atta boy," Gary said. He looked over at the others. "Reflex test," he explained. "You're looking for a blinking response, but you have to be careful about the way you move. You want to be sure he's blinking because he registered your finger, not because of the movement of air near his eye."

He moved to the other side and repeated the process. This time, AB didn't react.

"Did he blink?" Katie asked.

Gary frowned. "No, but that's not necessarily definitive. Can someone give me a hand here?" he asked. "Melissa, how about you, since you're the reason AB's getting all this special attention?"

Melissa stepped into the stall. "Sorry about this,

AB," she told the palomino. "I was just trying to help."

Gary pulled a vial of liquid out of his bag. "I just need you to hold him steady while I apply drops in his eyes. It'll only take a second."

"Is this like when the eye doctor dilates your pupils?" Katie asked.

"Yep," Gary said, removing the dropper from the bottle. "Of course, the pupil's shaped differently in a horse, but the principle's the same."

While Melissa held AB's head steady, cooing softly, Gary quickly applied the liquid to the horse's eyes. "Thanks, Melissa," he said. "You too, AB."

He returned the drops to his bag and removed a small hand-held instrument with a light at one end. "Now, we give those baby blues—sorry, AB—baby browns—a few moments to dilate, and then I use this little number to check them out. It's called an opthalmoscope, for those of you scoring at home."

"Have you found anything that might conceivably constitute enough evidence to convince Angie's parents she's been abusing AB?" Margaret asked.

"Nothing definite. There's this little abrasion over his eye, but that could easily have been caused by a branch on a trail."

"That's what Angie claims, but I'll bet she's lying," Melissa said darkly.

"Maybe, but it's hardly enough to prove her guilt." Gary gave a frustrated shrug. "Innocent until proven guilty. That is how we do things in this country."

He clicked on the light. "Now, just keep him nice

and steady while I check things out."

"Good boy," Melissa said softly as she steadied AB's head. "This doesn't hurt, now, does it?"

"Clear as a bell," Gary reported. "Looking good, AB. Let me do the other side and we'll give you a break from all this poking and prodding."

Gary and Melissa switched sides. "Okay," Gary murmured, shining the bright beam into AB's right eye, "you're doing fine, AB." He paused, brow furrowed. "Hmm."

"Hmm?" Margaret repeated.

"Hold him steady, Melissa," Gary said. "Hmm," he repeated again. "This is not good."

"What is it?" Melissa asked.

"See for yourself." Gary stepped back. "See that whitish veil of tissue coming toward you?"

Melissa nodded.

"That's a detached retina."

"Oh, no, Gary," Margaret said softly. "Are you sure?"

"Positive. We'll have to wait for the dilating solution to wear off before I can do some more reflex tests, but I'd be surprised if AB has much vision at all in that eye."

"What causes something like that?" Jenna asked.

"More often than not," Gary replied, "severe trauma to the eye area." He looked at Melissa. "I think we may just have come up with the proof we needed, at last. Too bad it had to happen this way."

"Oh, AB." Melissa buried her face in the horse's

smooth neck. "I'm so sorry. Maybe if I'd tried harder, if I'd noticed sooner—"

"Melissa, hon," Margaret said. "You did more than most people would have. You even risked your job. You should be proud of yourself."

Gary nodded. "Could be you've saved this horse from far worse trauma, too."

"But can he even be ridden now?" Katie asked, her brown eyes glistening.

"Sure," Gary said. "I've treated many horses who've lost sight in one eye and can still be used for pleasure riding. Of course, they're more likely to shy under certain circumstances—trail riding, or in an unfamiliar environment—so they need an experienced rider."

"And you have to be careful to make them aware of your presence when you're on their blind side," Margaret added.

"It's not like we're going to put you out to pasture yet, guy," Gary said, stroking AB at the base of his tail. AB nodded contentedly, indifferent to all the fuss.

"It's not fair," Melissa whispered. She stared into AB's right eye, the deep, unblinking brown, and shuddered.

The sharp click of heels on cement filled the stable. Melissa turned to see Mrs. Marquette striding toward them at a rapid clip, Angie by her side.

"I go to drop my daughter off for a nice day of riding, and two seconds later, she's running back to the car telling me there are a bunch of strangers crowded into AB's stall," Mrs. Marquette said. She shook her finger at Gary, gold bracelets jangling musically. "I don't recall authorizing a veterinary exam of this horse," she said. "And since you are not our regular vet, might I suggest you remove yourself from this stall before I have your license revoked?"

"Get her out of there, too," Angie demanded, glaring at Melissa.

"And as for you," Mrs. Marquette continued, "I was told you were fired. What is this obsession you seem to have with my daughter's horse?"

"Your daughter's horse," Melissa said, stroking AB's neck, "is blind in one eye, Mrs. Marquette. And your daughter is responsible."

The accusation hung in the air. AB stomped his hoof. Angie stared, transfixed, at her horse.

"It's not true," she said at last.

Her voice held a mixture of anger and fear. There was something else there, too, Melissa thought. Hope? Was Angie actually hoping they were wrong? Did she, at some level, still love AB? Was she feeling regret?

"This is nonsense," Mrs. Marquette said firmly. "That horse is a perfect specimen."

"AB has permanent retinal damage to his right eye, Mrs. Marquette," Gary said. "Almost certainly caused by severe trauma."

Angie took a step back. Her lower lip quivered slightly. "He . . . he hit his head on a branch or something. I didn't hit him, Mom, I swear . . ."

"I saw you beat him," Melissa said. "I saw you,

Angie. Who knows how many other times you did it when no one was around to see you?"

"It couldn't have . . . I didn't mean to . . ."

"Mrs. Marquette, I can't allow this horse to be entered in the Autumn Show," Gary said.

Mrs. Marquette fell silent. At last she reached for her daughter's shoulder. "Tell me the truth, Angie," she said in a harsh whisper.

Angie threw off her mother's arm. "I hate that damn horse," she shouted. Then she spun around and ran, boots clattering, down the aisle and out the door.

"Well." Mrs. Marquette smoothed her dress. She started to speak, then stopped herself. Instead she stepped into AB's stall. Gently, she ran her perfectly manicured fingers through his snowy mane. "He's all right, otherwise?" she asked, turning to Gary.

"As far as I can tell, except for a minor abrasion," Gary said. He lowered his voice. "I'm going to recommend that Angie be barred from the show, Mrs. Marquette. In my opinion she shouldn't be riding this horse, or any horse."

She lowered her head, a barely visible nod. As she turned to leave, her eyes met Melissa's for a brief, hard moment. "She really does love this horse," she said softly.

Without another word, she left them, heels clicking purposefully, as if she were late to a very important meeting.

Margaret nodded at Melissa. "See, Melissa? You did the right thing."

But as Melissa gazed into AB's dark, unseeing eye, she wondered how, having done the right thing, she could still feel so very wrong.

"I wish I could have done more, AB," she whispered.

He nuzzled her cheek as if to say, *I know you did your best.*

"Why are we having steak?" Thomas demanded that evening, staring into the oven.

"It's not steak, it's salmon," his mother replied.

Thomas grabbed his stomach. "Puke."

"Sometimes, my dear son, you have to take what you can get in this world."

"Think of it as steak that swims," Melissa counseled as she set the table.

"I like macaroni and cheese," Thomas said.

His mother handed him napkins for the table. "We'll have that tomorrow, and tomorrow, and, at the rate we're going, the tomorrow after that. But tonight we're celebrating. It's Melissa's favorite."

"What are we celebrating?" Thomas asked.

"We are celebrating the fact that your sister is a very cool kid. You are also cool," she added as Thomas opened his mouth to protest, "but you did not just risk your job to do something about cruelty you'd witnessed."

"I stopped Carl from mushing a worm on the way to school," Thomas said.

"Then this salmon is also in honor of you," Ms. Hall said. "I'm sure the worm is counting his blessings."

"Mom, I wish you'd let this drop," Melissa complained. "It's not exactly like there was a perfectly happy ending. AB's blind in one eye, and he's still owned by the Marquettes, and I'm still jobless."

"Still, he could have been a lot worse off, if you hadn't persisted."

The phone rang and Thomas ran to answer it. "Make it quick," Ms. Hall warned. "The salmon's almost ready."

"Melissa, for you." Thomas rolled his eyes as he passed her the receiver. "Make it quick, or your swimming steak will be char-broiled."

"Melissa? This is Rose. Sorry about the static. I'm on the portable phone in the barn. Do you want the good news first or the good news?"

"I thought it was good news or bad news."

"I don't have any bad news. Unless, of course, you think setting your alarm for four A.M. constitutes bad news."

"Why would I . . . wait a minute. Are you asking me to come back to work?"

"Asking, no. Begging is more like it." In the background, a horse whinnied. "Sorry," Rose said. "Big Red wanted to say hi. Melissa, darlin', you're the best thing that ever happened to this stable. It's never been so organized." Her raspy voice softened. "You do realize, I hope, I didn't want to have to let you go. I believed you from the start. But—"

"I understand, Rose. Really I do. And the answer is yes, absolutely yes. When do I start?"

"Bright and early Monday. By the way, have I mentioned that I'm very proud to have you at Silver Creek?"

"Thanks, Rose. I'll see you Monday morning—"

"Wait, wait. You forgot the other good news. We've added a new horse to the stable."

"Really? That's great. What's he like?"

"You'll meet him Monday. Sweet as they come. Calm, reliable. Nice, clean gaits." She paused. "Of course, he can't see worth a darn—"

Melissa gasped. "You didn't!"

"We did."

"You bought AB? But in a million years, I'd have never guessed Mrs. Marquette would sell him, especially to Silver Creek."

"I think the whole thing shook her up good. I called her this afternoon and told her Angie shouldn't have a horse till she can handle one properly. Then I offered her a fair price on AB, and, lo and behold, after a little arm-wrestling, she took me up on it."

"I'm so glad, Rose."

"Me too, hon. There's no telling what would have happened to that horse if it hadn't been for you."

"See you Monday," Melissa said softly. "And thanks, Rose."

"Thank you." Another horse whinnied. "Hear that? AB says thanks, too."

"Good news?" Melissa's mother asked as she pulled the salmon from the oven.

"Well, it seems AB has a new owner—Rose—and I

have my old job back," Melissa replied.

"That's wonderful!" her mother cried.

Thomas nodded. "Way to go, Lissa."

"It's not a perfectly happy ending, I guess." Melissa grinned. "But you know what? I'll take what I can get."

12

"Dad, can you please floor it?" Jenna asked.

Mr. McCloud rolled his eyes. "Keep talking like that and you won't have your license till you're thirty."

"As it is, we're going to be at the show grounds early," Sharon pointed out from the back seat.

"I'm sure Melissa will be glad to see us," Jenna said. "She and all the Silver Creek staff will already be there with the horses. This way we can help if they need it."

Katie yawned. "The good thing about getting up this early is I'm too sleepy to be nervous . . . yet, anyway."

Mr. McCloud looked in the rearview mirror. "I must say you three look very blue-ribbon chic. The breeches, the choker thingies, the . . . what is it you call those shirts? Mousetraps?"

"Ratcatchers, Dad." Jenna rolled her eyes. "Don't try to be funny this early. You'll strain your brain. At your age, that could be fatal. And we're counting on a ride home."

"Your concern is touching." Mr. McCloud turned down a broad avenue. Two big white pillars marked the entrance to the Willow Brook Riding Center, a large complex where several shows were held each year. "May I at least offer a bit of dadly advice?"

Jenna turned to the back seat occupants. "Vote."

"I vote yes. He was nice enough to drive us," Katie said.

"Sure." Sharon nodded. "But I bet you can't top my dad for cornball, Mr. Mc-C. He was practically crying this morning."

"Two to one, Dad," Jenna said. "You're on." She grinned. "But I already know what you're going to say."

"Fine." Her father laughed. "Why don't you tell me?"

Jenna cleared her throat. "You were going to say that it doesn't matter how well we do today, as long as we have a good time and learn something. That we're only competing against ourselves." She pursed her lips. "Oh, yeah. And the usual sentimental stuff about how proud you are."

Mr. McCloud pretended to wipe away a tear. "I'm deeply moved." He turned into the entrance. A large sign indicated the trailer parking area.

"Look!" Katie pointed toward the broad grassy field where the trailers sat in long rows.

"Boy, does this bring back memories," Sharon said softly.

They drove down a curved drive, and Mr. McCloud braked near one of the two large warm-up rings. Already a few riders were taking their horses over practice jumps.

"It's awfully early to be warming up, isn't it?" Katie asked.

Sharon nodded. "Depends on the horse, but you don't want to overwork him before a class. I used to walk my course, then take Cass out to a field for a little canter to work off some nerves. After that, I'd just pop her over a few jumps to get her nice and supple and that was it. She seemed to do best if I kept her pretty fresh. It depends, though." She watched a big chestnut gelding sail high over an oxer. "See how they overjumped that?"

"That's how Red is when he starts a course," Jenna says. "He's so playful and hyped up. It takes him a while to get down to business."

"That's why you should probably give him a pretty solid workout to get out all the kinks. With Say-So, though, Katie, I wouldn't overdo it."

"It's going to be so nice having an expert around to get us through this," Katie said.

"Don't forget you'll have Melissa, too," Sharon reminded her. "She's an old hand at these things."

"Don't worry, Dad." Jenna gave her father a kiss on the cheek. "With Sharon and Melissa around, Katie and I will be fine."

"Yeah," Sharon said quietly as she climbed out of the station wagon. "But who's going to get *me* through this day?"

"My last leg wrap," Melissa announced as she unwound the wrap from Say-So's rear leg. "Maybe we are making progress, after all."

"Melissa," Claire said as she hung a hay net in the temporary stall next door, "remind me to tell Mom to give you a raise. I don't know what we would have done without you this morning."

It *had* been quite a morning. To her surprise, Melissa had quickly become an indispensable part of the Silver Creek team, thanks, in great measure, to her organizational skills. All morning, the staff had thrown questions at her. Had she remembered the leg and tail wraps, the traveling blankets, the extra tack? Would she please remind Rose to bring the Coggins test and health exam certifications? Did she remember the hoof black, the rub rags, the extra water pails?

And then there was all the loading—smooth as silk, until it came to Big Red, who'd decided he really wasn't up for a show appearance. It had taken a joint effort requiring cajoling, begging, and enough sugar cubes to send a veterinary dentist into coronary arrest before Red had finally allowed himself to be loaded into the trailer.

At the show grounds, Melissa and Gordy had checked the temporary stalls, making sure the latches were secure and there were no dangerous nails or splinters that might harm the horses. Together they'd bedded the stalls with shavings, set up water pails, and hung hay nets. With Margaret and Rose, she'd gone to the show office to check in the Silver Creek team and pick up show programs and numbers.

Now, all that accomplished, it was time to put the

finishing touches on each of the horses, making sure they were groomed to absolute perfection.

Melissa stretched and yawned. She was tired already, but she didn't mind at all. She'd expected to wander around feeling useless today, or maybe even a little resentful. Instead, she was getting a whole different look at a show.

"Melissa!"

She turned to see Katie, Jenna and Sharon hurrying over, each carrying a garment bag containing their hunt coats and other supplies.

"We got here a little early so we could give you a hand," Katie said.

"Not early enough," Melissa replied, laughing. "Where were you two hours ago back at the stable, when I kept screwing up Blooper's tail braid?" She grinned at Sharon's worried expression. "Don't worry, Sharon, he looks great now. It's just that by my third tail, my fingers were starting to go numb."

Jenna gazed up at the gray quilt of clouds overhead. "I wish the weather would have cooperated a little more."

"Maybe it's an omen," Sharon said darkly.

"Sharon, everything's going to be fine. You should be excited," Melissa chided. She took the girls' garment bags and hung them on a hook outside Big Red's stall. "This is your triumphant return to the ring, remember?"

"I remember." Sharon reached for a show program. "Believe me, I remember."

Melissa exchanged a look with Jenna, who gave her a *who knows?* shrug.

Katie patted Sharon's shoulder. "Hey, Jenna and I are the ones who should be nervous. You're used to all this stuff."

"It's not nerves, it's . . ." Sharon tossed the program aside. She forced a grim smile. "I wish you were riding, too, Melissa," she said, changing the subject.

"You know, I don't mind as much as I thought I would." Melissa paused to sort through a bucket of grooming supplies. "Good, I did remember the hoof black," she said distractedly. She looked over at her friends. "Rose told me I could organize every show, if I wanted. I told her next show, I'd be riding again . . . I hope. But this is fun. I'm seeing it from the other side. I have a lot more appreciation for what the staff goes through."

Just then, Katie's face went stony. "Angie alert at two o'clock," she whispered.

A hundred yards away, Angie was threading between two of the Silver Creek trailers. She wore an oversized sweater over her white breeches and riding boots. Every so often, she stole a glance at the stalls.

"You don't think she's looking for AB, do you?" Melissa whispered. "She must know we didn't bring him."

"I wonder why she's wearing riding clothes," Jenna said.

"It's hard, letting go of riding all of a sudden,"

Sharon said. "I almost feel sorry for her."

"Don't," Katie said, her soft voice hardened. "She deserves what she got."

Melissa nodded. She felt both things, watching Angie slink away. Deep anger, for what she'd done to AB. And a horrible, sickening sadness for what Angie had lost because of her own cruelty.

"Here," she said, shaking off the gnawing anger. She handed the grooming bucket to Sharon. "You'd better get to work, you three. We've got horses to finish grooming. *Lots* of horses."

Sharon stood back to admire her handiwork. Blooper was tacked up and ready to rock. He looked impeccable, his coat shimmering, his hooves gleaming. She'd even applied a light coat of baby oil to the area around his muzzle and eyes to highlight the bay's delicate features. A silly touch, really, especially for a basic equitation class where it was the rider, not the horse, who was being judged. But she needed all the help she could get, Sharon figured. And besides, Blooper seemed to revel in all the attention. He really was a ham at heart.

The P.A. hissed. "Class Number 101, walk/trot for riders ages six to eight, will begin in thirty minutes." The voice floated over the grounds, lingering on the misty morning air. Sharon swallowed. Her class would be next.

Two stalls down, she found Jenna and Katie giving Say-So a final once-over. "He looks great, Katie,"

Sharon said. "Never better." She gave Say-So an affectionate rump pat. "I'm going to head on out to the warm-up ring. I guess I can't put this off any longer."

"Our class isn't for a while yet," Jenna said. "Want us to come give you moral support?"

"To tell you the truth, I could probably use a few minutes alone," Sharon admitted. "I'll catch up with you in a while, okay?"

"Okay," Jenna said, hesitating. "But we're going to be right there by the in-gate, cheering you on, whether you like it or not."

"I like," Sharon said.

"You're going to do great, Sharon," Jenna said, with such absolute confidence that for a moment Sharon almost believed her.

Sharon gave Say a last pat. "See you in a while," she said. She returned to Blooper's stall and was just leading him out when Katie appeared.

"Sharon?" she said, running her fingers over Blooper's meticulously braided mane. "Remember what you said when you gave that talk at PET that day? About how when you're on a horse, you get to move the way he does? The way you can't when you're just being a plain old person?"

"Don't remind me," Sharon said. "I've definitely decided against a career in public speaking."

"No, it was really great," Katie said. "I just wanted to tell you that I'm going to remember that when I'm riding Say-So in my class. What you said . . .

well, that's what really counts to me. That's what's special about riding." Katie brushed a stray tendril of long black hair out of her eyes. "For me, anyway. And I think"—she paused, stroking Blooper's flank— "I think you should remember it, too."

Sharon smiled. "I will. I promise."

"I'm definitely going back to PET next weekend to volunteer," Katie said. "Want to come? Jenna and Melissa said they would."

"I don't think so, Katie."

"You sure? The kids really loved—"

"I'm sure."

"Well." Katie stepped back. "Have a good warm up."

"We will."

Sharon climbed onto Blooper and rode him toward the busy warm-up ring. Already the grounds buzzed with that familiar air that was part circus-like frenzy, part calm, organized, tradition. All shows, whether casual schooling or A-rated AHSA, shared this feeling, Sharon thought. Behind the scenes all day, riders would weep and rejoice. They'd practice and plan and maybe even pray a little. There would be frantic searches for a lost hard hat or a much-needed lucky charm.

But when once they were in that show ring, no matter what happened, everything would be orderly, calm and systematic. There were rules, right ways and wrong ways, penalty points and numerical scores. Some of the judging were subjective; some, like the jumper classes, were tied to the clock. But it was all part of a long, grand tradition, a tradition Sharon had once been a part of.

And now, at last, she would be a part of it again.

This is a good thing, she told herself as she entered the warm-up ring. This is where I belong.

She nudged Blooper into a sitting trot. It was hard on her legs, but she hadn't stretched out this morning the way she should have, and it was a good way to loosen up her tight thigh muscles. She had to veer to keep from rear-ending a small bay hugging the rail at a walk. The horses at a slower gait should have stayed off the rail, but, as usual, the ring was a confused traffic jam of nervous riders, some of whom were not particularly concerned with ring etiquette.

She tried to visualize herself in the show ring, the way she used to do before a class with Cassidy. She'd walk her course, pacing off distances, anticipating the angle of a jump approach. Where would she need to lengthen Cassidy's stride? Where would she need to collect it? Would Cass be likely to rush through those verticals? Was that tight turn into the final combination going to give them trouble? She'd visualize them floating over jumps, the images so real she could practically feel the clutch in her heart as Cassidy's thundering approach gave way to the pure, silent rush as they went airborne.

These days, there was much less to visualize. Were her hands still? Was her contact with the horse's mouth even? Heels down? Shoulders back? Simple stuff, compared to the complicated mental arithmetic of a jump course.

And yet, as she began posting, Sharon couldn't seem to visualize any of those simple tasks. When she imagined herself in the show ring, she saw a too-old, too-clumsy rider, a rider who struggled with even the easiest skills.

What she imagined was humiliation.

Out of the corner of her eye, she registered a thin young woman with wavy dark hair rushing toward the fence, a notebook in one hand. Marta, it had to be.

"Sharon!" Marta climbed onto the rail. "This is so great! I've never been to a horse show before."

Sharon exited the ring and brought Blooper to a halt near Marta. "Are you . . . doing another story?" she asked warily.

"A follow-up, yeah." Marta pulled a pen out of her jeans pocket. "Just a little blurb, you know, to see how you do. And a wrap-up on the show."

"Marta." Sharon fiddled with her reins distractedly. "No one cares how I do."

"Boy, do you have that wrong. You wouldn't believe the calls we've had about that story I did. People were so impressed. They gobble up that human interest stuff." Marta patted Blooper gingerly on the neck. "He won't bite, will he?"

"Blooper? No. He's a sweetheart. And don't let his name mislead you. He's an old hand at shows. If anyone will live up to his name, it's me."

Marta began scribbling. "Great quote," she said.

"Just let me be sure I got that right. *If anyone will live up—*"

"Marta, I really need to get going. The walk/trot for six-to-eights is in a few minutes, and my class is after that."

"How about an interview afterwards, then? Jack's around here someplace. We could get a few shots of you and your mighty steed for the article."

"I don't think—"

"Sharon Finnerty!" A familiar voice cut through Sharon's thoughts. "I knew it had to be you. I'd know that hair anywhere!"

Lucinda James came bounding up. She was dressed in designer everything, right down to the unnecessary designer sunglasses. She peered over them, scanning Blooper critically, taking in Sharon's braces with a sigh. "Sharon." She patted Sharon's knee. "It hurts me so to see you this way."

"What way is that?" Sharon inquired.

Lucinda snatched her hand away and turned to Marta. "Hi," she said, noting the pen and pad Marta was holding. "I'm Lucinda James, an old friend of Sharon's. Are you with the *Gazette*, by chance?"

"Lucinda, this is Marta Aritas. What a coincidence, Marta," Sharon said, backing Blooper a couple steps. "You're looking for a human interest story, and I can't think of a more interesting human than Lucinda."

"So you two are old friends?" Marta asked.

"More like friendly competitors," Lucinda said.

"Competitors, anyway," Sharon amended.

"I came in third at the New England Classic behind Sharon and this black girl, what was her name?"

"Melissa Hall," Sharon said. "One of my best friends."

"Yeah, Melissa. Anyway, Sultan and I were having a bad day," Lucinda continued. "He's my Arabian."

"That's a horse?" Marta asked.

"Of course it's a horse," Lucinda snapped. "And well, anyway, I always hoped Sharon and I would have a rematch. But then . . . fate intervened."

"That old rascal fate." Sharon clucked her tongue. "He can be such a jerk sometimes."

"Still," Lucinda continued, "I'm sure Sharon will do well today. What was it you're entered in, again? Walk/trot/canter?"

"Walk/trot," Sharon said.

"Well," Lucinda said with a sympathetic nod, "I'm sure you'll work up to cantering. Someday, I'll bet you'll even be jumping again." She glanced at Sharon's leg. "You *can* jump, can't you?"

"I'm not sure. Stand real still and I'll give it a try."

Lucinda smiled nervously. "Sharon's always had a mouth on her," she said to Marta.

"That's my dry wit," Sharon explained. "Or is it my sweet inner charm? I always get those two mixed up." Sharon backed Blooper up a few more steps. "Well, I'd love to relive old times, but Blooper and I have work to do."

"Did you say Blooper?" Lucinda cried.

Sharon was already turning away, but in her mind's eye, she could see Lucinda's sneer.

She rode until she was sure she was in no danger of another run-in with anyone she knew. Already there was a fairly sizeable crowd in the stands. How many other people like Lucinda would be there, people who'd known her when she was that other rider, the other Sharon?

Off in the distance, she could see Jenna and Katie heading toward the warm-up ring. Katie waved, but Sharon pretended not to notice.

She turned Blooper sharply, away from the warm-up ring, from the show arena, from the crowds. She didn't know where she was going, but suddenly she knew with all her heart that she didn't belong here.

13

"Got a minute?"

Melissa leaned out of Foxy's stall. "Mom! What are you doing here?"

"I've never missed one of your shows. I'm not about to start now."

"But I'm not in this show."

Her mother swept out her hand. "What do you call all this hard work?"

Melissa checked Foxy's tail braid one more time, then latched the stall door. "It's not the same," she said, giving her mother a hug. "But I'm still glad you came. Thomas here?"

"He's at the refreshment stand, hoping to be their first official customer of the day. Which is good, because I wanted to give you this alone." She reached into her purse and fished around. "Here," she said, handing Melissa a tiny box wrapped in silver paper.

"What's this for?" Melissa asked.

"No reason."

"There has to be a reason," Melissa insisted.

"My logical daughter." Ms. Hall rolled her eyes. "All right. Let's just say it's for measuring up well at a time of challenge."

Melissa fingered the little silver bow. "The King quote."

"Exactly. Are you going to open it, or just admire my wrapping skills?"

"You shouldn't have spent the money, Mom," Melissa said as she tore off the paper.

"Well, if it makes you feel any better, I didn't spend a cent."

Melissa lifted the lid and dug beneath the layer of fluffy cotton. In the center she discovered a silver pin crusted with tiny diamond chips. "Mom," she whispered. "It's beautiful."

"Do you know what it is?"

Melissa lifted the pin from its cotton bedding. "It looks a little like a horseshoe."

"I thought so, too. But it's actually a wishbone. It was Grandma Tyler's. When she gave it to me, she told me I could wish on it and have anything I wanted—as long as I'd truly earned it." She put her arm around Melissa. "Well, I think you've earned a lot, Melissa. This hasn't been an easy time for you, and you've really made me proud to be your mom."

"Know what?" Melissa whispered. "I'm kind of proud to be your daughter, too."

Her mother took the wishbone and pinned it to Melissa's shirt. "Even though I'm unemployed?"

"Hey, you're my mom. Tell me that's not a job and a half."

Just then Jenna and Katie came running up. "Hey,

Ms. Hall," Jenna said breathlessly. "Have you seen
Sharon, Melissa?"

"I thought she was going to the warm-up ring,"
Melissa said. "Her class is up next."

"We just saw her there," Katie said anxiously.
"But all of a sudden she took off on Blooper and
disappeared."

"Maybe she just wanted to loosen up a little,"
Melissa suggested.

"Maybe," Jenna said doubtfully. "But Marta told us
she'd been talking to that Lucinda girl right before."

Melissa frowned. "Uh-oh. Lucinda could make
anybody want to disappear."

"We're going to go look for her. Have you got time
to help?"

"Of course," Melissa said. She turned to her mother.
"Thanks, Mom—"

"You go find Sharon," she said. "But before you do,
don't forget to make a wish."

Melissa touched the little pin and closed her eyes.
A moment later, she opened them. "Know what?"
she said. "I think I'll save it for something really
important." She gave her mother a long, hard hug.
"Right now I have everything I need."

Sharon made a wide arc around the show grounds,
trotting along on Blooper without worrying too much
about where they were going. The important thing
was, she knew where they *weren't* going. They weren't

going into the show ring. Not today. Not ever.

As she cut a path around the parking lot, she wondered what Marta would do for her article now. She could see the headline:

SILVER CREEK STABLES RIDER CHICKENS OUT

No, Marta would pretty it up somehow. She'd write up something about how Sharon had decided the time wasn't right for her triumphant return to the ring.

And that would be Sharon's story, too. She'd tell her friends the same thing—she wasn't quite ready. Maybe the next show, or the next.

She found herself skirting a row of temporary stalls, far enough from the Silver Creek contingent for her not to have to worry about running into anyone. She slowed Blooper to a walk and wove her way along. The crowd was growing. Riders dressed in their show finery ran to and fro purposefully, trainers and owners shouted directions, parents and friends wandered about.

Sharon checked her watch. Fifteen minutes until her class. She'd have to keep a low profile till then. If she ran into anyone from Silver Creek, they'd try to talk her out of her decision.

Near the last stalls, a small boy caught her eye. He was on crutches and wore braces on his lower legs. He moved along painstakingly slowly, his eyes glued to the stalls.

It wasn't until she got closer that Sharon recognized him. "Hey," she called. "You! BMX!"

The boy turned with difficulty. When he saw Sharon on Blooper, he smiled broadly.

"I thought you hated horses," Sharon said as she walked Blooper over.

The boy looked up at her. "I do. For one thing, they stink. Have you noticed?"

"It's like French perfume to me. What are you doing here, anyway?"

The boy shrugged. "No reason."

"You just happened to show up at a horse show, even though you don't want to have anything to do with horses?"

"My mom brought me. She's in the stands. I told her I wanted to check things out. She was trying to have quality time with me so I had to cut loose."

Sharon climbed down off Blooper. "You got a name?"

"Kurt."

"You mind if I walk with you for a while, Kurt?"

He frowned. "Don't you have a walk/trot class in a few minutes?"

"Hold it." Sharon gazed at him skeptically. He poked at a stone with his right crutch. "How come you know what class I'm in? Not to mention what time it starts?"

Kurt ignored her. He eyed Blooper doubtfully. "Is he a good horse?"

"Blooper's the best. Go ahead. Pet him."

"Nah."

"Bloop, say hi to Kurt." Gently Sharon guided

Blooper's head lower until he and Kurt were eye to eye.

Kurt reached up, touched Blooper's muzzle, then jerked back his hand.

"Soft, huh?" Sharon said.

"I'd rather have a BMX."

Sharon put her hands on her hips. "So what's the deal with you, Kurt? You never did answer my question."

"Look, I don't know why you're making a federal case," Kurt replied. "My mom saved that article about you and it said you were coming here. So I wanted to see how you did, okay? So is that some kind of crime?"

Sharon hesitated. "You came here to see me?"

"Yeah," Kurt said, glaring at her. "I thought it might be good for a laugh. You know, see you fall on your butt."

"Too bad." Sharon gave a brittle laugh. "Turns out I'm not going to be in the show, after all. Sorry you won't get to see me make a fool of myself."

"You're not . . . you mean you're not going to ride?" Kurt asked incredulously.

"Nope." Sharon fiddled with Blooper's mane.

"But how come?" Kurt demanded.

"How come do you think?" Sharon shot back. "Because I don't want a bunch of people laughing at me while I fall on my butt."

Kurt stared at her, eyes narrowed. "What?" Sharon demanded irritably. "What do you care?"

"I don't. Believe me." He began walking again,

lurching forward, then catching himself on his crutches.

For some reason she didn't understand, Sharon followed him. "So," she said. "I've got some time to kill. You want to ride Blooper?"

"No way."

"You don't know what you're missing," Sharon persisted.

"Forget it." Kurt veered to the left, away from the crowded path.

"The thing is, Blooper's like a big dog, he's so sweet. I promise you won't get hurt."

Kurt rounded on her. "Would you give it up, already?"

She was surprised to see the tears in his eyes. "Look, I'm sorry," Sharon said gently. "I didn't mean to pressure you. It's just . . . riding's so great. Especially when, you know, you have legs like ours." She shrugged. "And it just seemed fair."

"Fair, how?"

"Well, I've been on a bike before. But you've never been on a horse. I don't see how you can make a fair comparison unless you try them both."

Kurt stared at her with something very close to hatred in his eyes. "Have you been on a bike since your accident?"

"Well, no. Of course not."

"Why not?"

"It'd be too hard, with the braces. Knowing me, I'd fall off and end up . . ." Her voice trailed off. Suddenly she felt very weary. "Okay," she said. "I see your point. Forget it. I don't even know why I cared one way or the other." She turned to go. "Well, anyway. See you around."

She'd gone several feet before Kurt called to her. "You should go be in the show," he said firmly.

Sharon looked back. "And why, exactly, is that?"

"Because . . . because you're good. You won't fall on your butt. You're the best rider I've ever seen at PET."

Sharon had to keep herself from laughing. "Thanks, but that wouldn't count for much here, Kurt."

"Why not?"

"Well, it's hard to explain. But you have to be a better rider than the riders at PET to compete in a show like this."

Kurt furrowed his brow, as if she'd just addressed him in Greek. "But there are all kinds of riders here, right? And some are better than others, right?"

"Well, sure, but—"

"So I don't get why you can't be one of them."

Sharon sighed deeply. "Because I'm not like I used to be, Kurt. I used to be . . . well, I used to be pretty awesome, actually. I mean, when I rode Cassidy, it took people's breath away, mine included. But now, to be perfectly honest, nobody wants to see someone like me ride."

Kurt shook his head. "I do."

"Thanks, but—"

"You know, I could have gone to watch a bike race

today over at the state park," he said bitterly. "But no. I had to come here, to see the great Sharon Finnerty. Only she's too chicken-livered to go through with it—"

"You mean you really did come here just to see me?" Sharon asked, as the reality slowly penetrated. "Your mom didn't make you come?"

"No, my mom didn't make me come. Give me a break. I'm ten and half. She hasn't made me do anything since I was eight." Kurt shrugged. "What a waste of time. I should have known you'd freak—"

"Hold it. Are you trying to motivate me by infuriating me?"

"Is it working?" Kurt asked. "My p. t. tries it on me all the time."

In the distance, Sharon heard someone calling her name. She turned to see Katie, Jenna and Melissa running toward her. "Oh, wonderful," she muttered. "Just what I need. More motivation."

With a sigh, Sharon rubbed her cheek against Blooper's neck. At last she turned back to Kurt. "Look, if you came to see me ride, you're going to have to burn rubber to get back to the stands in time."

"You're riding?"

"Yeah, I suppose so, but don't go thinking you had anything to do with it. If my little brother ever finds out I let a ten-year-old influence me, he'll make my life miserable."

Sharon checked her watch. "You know, you're not going to make it back in time unless you climb on this horse and let me walk you over."

"No way."

"Does the phrase 'chicken-livered' ring a bell?"

"Sharon!" Jenna cried as she dashed up with Katie and Melissa close behind. "We've been looking all over for you. Where have you been?"

"Having a philosophy debate with Kurt here. Which do you think is better? Blooper or a BMX?"

"Sharon, you really need to hurry," Melissa urged.

"What's a BMX?" Katie asked.

"Only the most amazing bike ever created," Kurt replied.

"I mean, a bike doesn't smell," Sharon continued. "But it doesn't whinny when it sees you, either—"

"Do you *realize* what time it is?" Jenna cried in exasperation.

"Answer the question," Sharon insisted, grinning at Kurt.

"Okay, okay. Blooper, hands down," Jenna said.

"Bloop," Katie agreed.

Melissa nodded. "Blooper, easy."

Sharon crossed her arms. "Well?"

Kurt grimaced. "All right, already. I'll ride the stupid horse."

"Would you guys mind giving my friend here a leg up?" Sharon asked.

Kurt glared at her. "Don't go thinking you had anything to do with this," he warned. "If my big sister ever gets wind of this, she'll never let me live it down."

"Let's get going," Sharon said. "You came here to see a show."

14

"There," Melissa said, pointing to the show program. "Class 203, Hunters Over Fences, Fourteen and Under. That's Jenna's class. She's already on-deck, see?"

Ms. Hall nodded. "Isn't that the horse you rode in the camp show?"

"Big Red. He's a great jumper. Jenna should do well."

Melissa scanned the course, walking through it in her mind as if she were the one sitting nervously on Big Red waiting to hear her number called. A brush, followed by a couple of nice, low cross rails and then a pink and gray Swedish oxer. That would get her off to a good start. The only trouble might come later at the in-and-out, judging from the tight turn it would require to get a straight-on approach.

One more time, Melissa worked her way through the course of eight jumps. Jenna would be fine, she decided. No sweat.

She sighed. She would have to get back to the stalls soon. There would be bridles to change, horses to untack and cool down, last-minute crises to attend to. It had been a full day and Silver Creek still had riders entered in several other classes. By the time she got all the horses settled in for the night back at the stable, she was going to be bone-tired.

The first rider, a girl on a gray warmblood from nearby Canterbury Farms, rushed through the first two fences, then went off-course and forgot the third cross rail altogether. It wasn't until she'd nearly finished the course that she seemed to realize her mistake.

Poor kid, Melissa thought. She'd had days like that, too. And, Melissa reminded herself, she'd have more, soon enough. Good show days when she'd go home with a pocketful of ribbons, and bad days when she'd go home with regrets, vowing to work on something that had given her trouble in the show ring.

Today, all she'd be taking home were some great memories and some aching muscles. She'd expected to feel wistful, jealous, maybe even a little bitter. Instead she felt oddly satisfied.

Melissa ran her fingers over the wishbone pin. Then she reached for her mother's hand and gave it a squeeze.

"Number seven, Big Red, ridden by Jenna McCloud, owned by Silver Creek Stable." The announcer's voice boomed across the ring.

Jenna urged Big Red into a collected trot. As she moved through the in-gate into the ring, Melissa held her breath.

Jenna was the one riding, but in her own mind, Melissa was right there with her.

Clutching her green sixth-place ribbon, Katie watched as Jenna made an opening circle before she took Big Red over the first jump, a low brush he flew over with plenty of room to spare.

It was beautiful—flawless, from Katie's perspective—but then, of the four Silver Creek Riders, she was the newcomer to riding, the one who still asked silly questions and made silly mistakes. Sometimes she wondered if her riding would ever match the skill level of her friends. Would she always be behind the curve, hoping to catch up?

She ran her fingers over the glossy green ribbon. Her first AHSA show, her first class, her first ribbon, unless you counted the camp show.

Jenna had taken a third. Jenna probably would have placed even higher, but she'd been so nervous when all twelve riders had first entered the ring that she'd missed the judge's instruction to begin a rising trot. Once she'd settled down and focused, she'd performed perfectly.

Of course, Katie reminded herself, she hadn't done half bad herself. After all, she hadn't even expected to place. And here she was, holding a ribbon, what could be—could be—the first of many ribbons.

She knew just where she'd put it, too. On her dresser mirror, so that each time she gazed at her reflection, she would see a different Katie. Not the newcomer to riding who asked silly questions and made silly mistakes, but the rider who was improving with each lesson. The ribbon winner.

She held her breath as Red approached the oxer. Had Jenna shortened his stride before takeoff? How did she manage to find their distance so perfectly?

There were so many questions, silly or not, to ask. So many things to learn. It filled Katie with a giddy, exhilarating sense of possibilities. Someday soon that would be her, sailing over those jumps.

But in the meantime, this was enough, being right there with Jenna—in spirit, at least. Katie sat on the edge of her seat, biting her lip, crossing her fingers, forgetting to breathe, all the while clutching her shiny green ribbon.

Sharon chewed on her thumbnail as Jenna approached the in-and-out. She was pushing it a little hard, losing what up till now had been a perfectly rhythmic stride. But she collected Red in time, and he took the first half of the combination like a pro. Jenna recovered her position immediately, and two strides later, Red was up again, front legs folded high and evenly, tracing a graceful arc over the second vertical.

"Yes!" Sharon said under her breath. "Way to go, Jen."

Out of the corner of her eye she spotted Lucinda a few rows below, watching Jenna while she sipped at a soft drink. Jenna guided Red over the next fence, and

Lucinda gave a tiny nod of approval.

Sharon felt a surge of satisfaction and pride, almost as if she were the one in the ring, not Jenna. In the old days, it had been Sharon and Cassidy solo, competing against their own record or against an old rival. But today, for the first time, Sharon felt like part of a whole team. Already, Rose had reported, the stable had more than a dozen ribbons to their credit, and more, undoubtedly were on the way.

Sharon reached into her coat pocket. Her pink fifth place ribbon was crammed in the bottom, along with a piece of Kleenex, an extra safety pin, and a Kit-Kat wrapper. She had stuffed the ribbon away unceremoniously, ignoring her friend's cheers when the judge had awarded it to her. It was, after all, a fifth in a class of beginning riders. It was meaningless. Embarrassing, really.

Sharon glanced over at Katie. Her eyes were trained on Jenna and Big Red. In her right hand, Katie clutched the green ribbon she'd won in the walk/trot/canter class. Katie had been so proud of that ribbon. She'd ridden out of the ring with the same inspired expression of someone who'd just experienced her first roller coaster ride.

Well, she should be thrilled. Katie was a good rider, and she was going to be a great rider someday. Taking a sixth in your first accredited show was something worth celebrating.

Slowly Sharon pulled the pink ribbon from her pocket. There was a little chocolate stain on the bottom, but it was otherwise okay. There would be more ribbons like this, she supposed. Not as many as she'd like, probably, and they'd be hard-earned, every one of them.

She probably shouldn't have treated it so badly. It was an important ribbon. Maybe even the most important ribbon in her riding career. It deserved a place of honor. Something better, at least, than the bottom of her pocket.

Suddenly she smiled. She knew just where it belonged.

Sharon looked up just in time to see Jenna and Red approaching their last jump, a gate. "There you go, Jenna, nice and easy," she whispered, and then she held her breath and waited for the take-off, almost as if she were riding Red herself.

"One more," Jenna whispered, pulling Red up just slightly. She could feel him anticipating the gate as he bounded toward it, surging against her grip, ears pricked forward. Jenna fastened her gaze on the center of the fence, keeping Red's approach smooth and straight on. She got into position, giving him his head, and Red took off like he'd been powered by NASA.

It was a beautiful jump, she was sure of it, the best they'd done on the course. She didn't care any more how the judges scored their ride. She knew she'd done her best. She knew Red had done his best. And all of a sudden, to her surprise, that seemed like plenty.

As she headed for the out-gate, she heard the cheers from the stands. She turned to wave, and was rewarded with the sight of her friends from Silver Creek, all of them waving silver scarves in the air.

Jenna reached down to pat Red's hot, damp neck. "You made me look good, guy," she said gratefully. Red gave a triumphant toss of his beautiful head, as if he were already certain of their victory.

She was cooling Red down a few minutes later when Melissa, Katie and Sharon finally caught up with her.

"Amazing," Melissa said, beaming.

Katie patted her leg. "I hope I can do that someday, Jen."

"Me, too," Sharon added with a grin. "You looked great out there, Jenna. I was so proud."

"I pushed it a little coming into that oxer," Jenna said doubtfully. "And on the in-and-out—"

"Would you stop second-guessing yourself? It was beautiful," Sharon said.

The P.A. hissed. "First prize, Hunters Over Fences, Fourteen and Under, goes to Jennifer Byron on Easy Money."

"She owns that gorgeous Thoroughbred," Jenna said as she dismounted. "That was a great ride, did you see?" She nodded toward the field behind the ring. "You guys coming? I'm going to walk Red out for a few minutes."

"Wait a minute," Melissa cried. "You're leaving *now*?"

"Aren't you even remotely curious about who places?" Katie demanded.

"Well, let's face it, that was a big class. It's not like I'm in any danger of taking home another ribbon," Jenna said. "And I can hear the announcer out there, anyway—"

"Jenna." Sharon shook her by the shoulders. "You really don't realize how well you did, do you?"

"Second prize goes to Jenna McCloud on Big Red," the P.A. blared.

Jenna blinked. She looked at her friends doubtfully. Her name echoed through the ring. In the stands, she could see her parents, her little sister, Rose, Claire, Margaret and Gary cheering.

"I think maybe I'm having some kind of brain malfunction," Jenna said. "I know this is crazy, but I could have sworn they just said—"

"Jenna, climb back on that horse and go accept your ribbon, or *I'll* do it for you," Melissa ordered.

Jenna mounted Big Red and rode to the judges' stand. But even when she saw the red ribbon, even later when she held it and stared at it and passed it around, it didn't quite feel like it belonged to her.

Somehow, in a way she couldn't quite explain, it belonged to Melissa and Katie and Sharon, too. To her friends who'd rooted for her in the stands, holding their breath and waving their silver scarves.

15

The kids were already streaming into the PET stable by the time Sharon and her friends arrived the following Saturday. Kurt caught up with Sharon while she was tacking up Spot.

"Hey," he said nonchalantly.

"Hey," she responded.

"I saw you in the paper. Bad picture. But I liked the headline. *Fifth-Place Finnerty A Winner Nonetheless*."

"It was a lousy picture," Sharon admitted. "But Blooper looked great. You riding today?"

"Maybe."

"You did great on Blooper that day at the show."

"I said maybe, okay?"

Sharon rechecked Spot's girth. "I was hoping you'd show up. I've got something for you." She reached into her jeans pocket and passed the pink ribbon to Kurt.

He stared at it for a long time without uttering a sound.

"I figured I kind of owed it to you, since you talked me into going through with the show," Sharon said.

Still he didn't speak.

"Look, I know it's kind of stupid."

Kurt frowned. "There's chocolate on it," he said at last.

"Kit-Kat."

"And it's pink," he pointed out. "That's like a major girl color."

"Sorry. Maybe next time it'll be blue."

Kurt stuffed the ribbon in his jeans pocket. "Yeah, well, thanks," he said with a shrug.

Sharon watched him as he made his way slowly back down the aisle. "Jeez," she said to Jenna. "What a moving moment." She rolled her eyes. "You know what? I'm lousy with kids. Why'd you talk me into coming back here?"

"Because we're your friends, and we know what's good for you," Jenna said.

Katie came down the aisle, frowning. "What's with Kurt?" she asked.

"What are you talking about?" Sharon asked. "He's fine."

"No, I'm pretty sure he was crying," Katie said.

Jenna smiled at Sharon. "Maybe you're better with kids than you think."

"Maybe so," Sharon said thoughtfully. She clucked to Spot and led him out of his stall. "Come on, old friend," she said. "There's somebody I'd like you to meet."

For information on volunteer opportunities at a therapeutic riding program, contact the North American Riding for the Handicapped Association at 1-800-369-RIDE.

CLUB Sunset Island™

Join Dixie, Tori, Becky and Allie for an incredible summer as counselors-in-training at Club Sunset, the new day camp on Sunset Island!

__TOO MANY BOYS!   0-425-14252-3/$3.50
A whole boat full of cute boys is beached on Sunset Island–and Becky and Allie have to get ready for Parents' Day.

__DIXIE'S FIRST KISS   0-425-14291-4/$3.50
It's the camp's rafting trip and Dixie's finally going to get the chance to spend some time with Ethan Hewitt...if only Patti will leave her alone.

__TORI'S CRUSH   0-425-14337-6/$3.50
Tori's tired of being called a tomboy, but now her athletic abilities may catch the eye of one of the counselors, Pete Tilly.